THE UNWI

Ravena loved her childhood friend and
sweetheart, Rhodri Brenin – but she
had married a virtual stranger, the forbidding Sardinian Mark di Curzio, for
whom she had no feeling but apprehension. Why?

THE
UNWILLING BRIDE

BY

VIOLET WINSPEAR

MILLS & BOON LIMITED

15–16 BROOK'S MEWS
LONDON W1A 1DR

First published 1970
Australian copyright 1981
Philippine copyright 1977
This edition 1981

© Violet Winspear 1970

ISBN 0 263 72408 5

*Printed and bound in Great Britain by
Cox & Wyman Ltd, Reading*

CHAPTER ONE

THE bridegroom placed his hand over the bride's on the hilt of her guardian's sword and as they cut the wedding cake there were congratulatory cheers, the clink of champagne glasses, laughter.

"Is it a fact," someone asked the groom, "that the men of your country slap the bride on their wedding day to let them know who's boss?"

"You speak of Sicily," smiled Mark di Curzio. "I am a Sard."

He was answering questions about Sardinia when another of the guests handed a small yellow envelope to the bride. "This just came, Ravena. Another good luck message, I expect."

Her smile was slightly strained as she opened and read the telegram, then she glanced quickly at Mark. He had not seen her perusal of it and it took but a second to thrust it down the side of one of her satin slippers. She was so pale that her eyes had the gleam of green jewels.

At last came the moment for her to go upstairs and change for the honeymoon journey. She declined the offer of the friend who wanted to help her. "I – I want to be alone," she said, and hoped she didn't look as desperate as she felt.

It didn't take her long to change out of her wedding dress of pale gold, with a veil of old Welsh lace, and clad in her going-away suit she stood in the window recess of her room and stared at the elm tree that overhung the garden below. With nostalgia she thought of Rhodri climbing the tree and perching in its boughs. One day he would be her knight gallant, another day he would have the devil in him and tease her.

She and Rhodri had grown up together in this time-worn house on the Welsh border. He was the only son of Colonel Caruth Brenin, her guardian for so many years that she thought of him as almost a parent – a much loved one.

About eighteen months ago Rhodri had resigned his commission in the Army and gone away to farm in New South Wales. It had been a blow to Guardy, with his own distinguished military career, but Ravena had been unsurprised by Rhodri's defection. It was because he came of a military line, the tradition ranging far back into Welsh history, that he had felt compelled to follow his father into the Army. Ravena knew there was a restless streak in Rhodri Brenin.

After receiving his commission he had been assigned to a special mission in Cyprus. Guardy's pride had known no bounds, though he fretted that his son should spend his leave abroad.

It was soon after his leave that Rhodri had left the Army.

Ravena stared from her bedroom window and seemed to hear again the ring of a horse's hooves on the cobbles of the garden court. She had been tidying up in the library when she heard the hooves, and then the sound of booted feet coming along the terrace that bordered the library windows. She recalled her start of alarm as the tall figure of Mark di Curzio darkened the glass doors.

They had stared at each other through the glass, then without invitation he had stepped into the library. "Good afternoon, Miss Brenin." As he gave her that brief foreign bow of his, she sensed the vibration in the air, felt by her whenever he came to dine at Ravenhall.

He was a business associate of Guardy's, but this was the first time they had been alone. He lived abroad. That was all she knew, for the man was aloof, older than her own friends, with an air of mystery about him.

He was very erect and yet he gave an impression of great suppleness as he came towards her. Her teeth bit down hard on her bottom lip as she saw once again the left side of his face, ravaged as if by fire. She glanced away. It was as if the face of the devil and an angel had been joined together!

"I hope you have been keeping in good health, Ravena," the accent on the final syllable of her name.

She tensed at his use of her first name. There was a quality about the man that put her on the defensive. "I'm afraid my guardian is out," she said in a cool voice.

"I came to see you!"

His words came as a shock and she stared at the haughty face that had once been strikingly handsome. There was a dark force about the man, unfathomable depth to the eyes that were so dark the pupils merged with the iris.

She touched the flowers in a vase on the table, as if their softness might deflect some of the hardness of the man. Wild flowers she had plucked from the roadside on her way home from shopping in the village.

"I came at this particular hour because I knew your guardian would not be at home. This is the afternoon when he plays bowls with Ewen Carew, an old Army comrade, is it not?"

"I hardly know you, Signor di Curzio! I can't think of anything we have to discuss." She faced him, her

7

dark red hair straight as her glance, fine as the set of her grey-green eyes.

"You will know me better in a while." His smile was a twist of the lip, and he indicated a pair of deep chairs with hollowed leather seats. "Please let us be seated, or I shall think that you wish to run away from me."

Her nerves tightened and she had an impulse to tell him to leave Ravenhall this instant! He met her eyes and she knew he read her thoughts. "I can give you only a few minutes," she said stiffly. "I do the cooking and Guardy is used to having his evening meal on time."

"Please sit down, *signorina*."

She did so and he followed suit. He crossed his legs and the light caught the polished leather of his knee-boots. His breeches and his tweed jacket were too well tailored to be anything but British made. He didn't carry a riding-whip, too sure of his control over his mount – and people – to be in need of a whip.

"May I smoke?" he asked.

She nodded and watched him extract a small, thin cigar from a well-handled leather case. He lit the cigar with a match and the flame was almost at his fingertips before he tossed it into the fireplace. The big grate was empty, for summer was edging its way into the English weather.

"I always feel the cold when I come to England," he said. "The sun shines more moderately here than over in my country."

"Really, *signore*?" She looked polite but had no inclination to ask him where he came from; she wanted him to speak his piece and then go. He disturbed her, more than ever now they were alone, and she wanted this enforced intimacy to be over as soon as possible.

8

"Come, *signorina*," he looked faintly mocking, "don't be so British and controlled, ask me outright why I waylay you like this in your own home."

"We're comparative strangers, so it can't be anything important," she said in her coolest voice. "But I see that you mean to make me listen to you."

"I came to tell you a story, Miss Brenin."

"A *story*?" She half rose from her chair, then sank back as he seemed to pin her there with his dark, glinting eyes. They took in her every feature, and dwelt on the tiny mole just below her left eye – a dark tear forever in the act of falling. Her fingers closed hard on the arms of her chair.

"I'm listening, *signore*. Please begin your – story!"

"I am a widower." He flicked cigar ash into the fireplace, but his glance did not leave her face. "My young wife Donata died when our son was born and I transferred all my love and hope to that small boy. Dresti, warm-skinned, active and affectionate in the way of most children ... until eighteen months ago when a drunken driver ran into my car, in which Dresti was asleep beside me."

He paused, as if to let the words sink into Ravena. "Yes, I crashed, Miss Brenin, and the other man drove on and left my car overturned and in flames."

Ravena put a hand to her cheek, an instinctive gesture of shock as her eyes dwelt on Mark di Curzio's fire-scarred face.

"My son and I were trapped," he went on harshly. "I fought like one insane to force a window, to get my son out of the car – *Per Dio*, if that reckless criminal had stopped and helped, my son might be alive today!"

"*Oh, no!*" Ravena couldn't bear the thought of a small boy dying in that way.

9

"The petrol tank exploded," he continued inexorably, "and I was thrown burning into a field where vineyard workers beat out the flames, Miss Brenin. They were far across the field and could not reach the car before it exploded – only the man who drove into us could have been of assistance. A man whose identity I traced after long months in hospital, through the garage that repaired the car he was driving, hired for a holiday by a man named Captain Rhodri Brenin of the British Army on a special posting in Cyprus!"

The eyes of Mark di Curzio held a bitter reproach as they dwelt on Ravena's face, gone so white that her mouth looked bruised.

"Your guardian's son caused the death of my son." The words seemed to fill the air of the room with tangible pain and anger. "Dresti was four years old. The child was my wife's last gift of love to me. The son who would have inherited my land and my property and carried on a name which has been honoured in Sardinia for many, many years. The word honour has meaning for all Sards, and so, I believe, for men like Colonel Caruth Brenin."

"Guardy?" she exclaimed. "You mean – you intend to tell him that Rhodri was drunk while driving, and that he caused your car to crash? You can't!" She jumped to her feet. "It would kill him!"

"In my country," Mark di Curzio got to his feet, "an injury, or a dishonour, is paid for by the family of the culprit. We believe, you see, that when a man goes wrong his family is to blame in some measure."

"But this is England!" She couldn't believe that any man, no matter how badly hurt in heart and body, could make a kind, elderly, campaign-worn soldier take the blame for his son's misdeed. "We – we try to forgive, *signore*. We don't ask someone else to pay for a wrong-doing."

"I am a Sard. For eighteen months I have asked myself what would be a just price for a member of this house to pay – and today I have the answer."

"You mean to hurt my guardian?"

"Not necessarily, Miss Brenin."

"But you implied – " She stared at the man and would have felt hopeful if he had not looked so stern and dark. A man in whose blood ran the vendettas of a proud, passionate, dangerous people. Sards! Guardy had talked about a regiment of them, who had fought like demons against the Austrians in the First World War. Men who had formed their own *maquis* in the second great war.

"Your guardian need never know about the son who proved himself a coward," said Mark di Curzio, deliberately.

"How – ?"

The clock ticked with torturing calmness as she waited for him to speak. There was a quality of stillness about him that made her think of a panther – tensed to spring on its prey. The silence between them held the warning of a pounce.

"You will marry me," he said quietly. "You will give me a son for the one I lost."

Ravena could hardly believe that she heard him correctly. She couldn't speak, and then the words came with a rush. "You can't be serious!"

"I have never been more serious," he replied.

"I – it's mad! I could never marry you!"

"You think not?" His smile twisted his lip, as if her feelings hardly counted in the matter. "Love will force you to marry me."

11

"*Love?*" She felt a rush of ice through her body, and when she moved as if to run from the sight of him – scarred, with eyes and brows black as night – he stepped in front of her, barring the way.

"Do you imagine I could ever love *you*?" In her fear she used the female weapon of scorn.

"No, my imagination is not that powerful," he mocked. "But you love your guardian. You would not have him hurt, or disillusioned by the son *he* loves."

"You are very cruel, Signore di Curzio!"

"I never used to be, *signorina*. A man named Rhodri Brenin made me so." The dark eyes looked into hers, hard and merciless, and her heart told her one way or another the house of Brenin would be made to pay for the cruel way he had lost his young son.

"What would you gain, *signore*, married to a woman who doesn't love you?" She tried to speak reasonably, despite the foreboding thuds of her heart. "What if I said I loved another man?"

"Do you?" His eyes took in her hair, which was looped back in a ribbon while she did her housework. Rather wonderful hair, a smouldering dark red.

"It's my affair," she said defiantly.

"On the contrary," he tossed the end of his cigar into the fireplace, "as my wife you will have to forget this other man."

"Y-you really mean to force me into marrying you?" Suddenly she felt frightened, bewildered, and could not help but show it in her green eyes.

His brief bow spoke for him. "In the past few weeks I have learned a lot about you, Miss Brenin, especially about your devotion to the Colonel of Guards who has been like a father to you. Devotion is something I admire in a woman, being a Sard. Loyalty is what I will accept in place of love."

"You came ready to set your foot on someone's neck," she exclaimed, "and it's to be mine! I must bow down to you because you know that Guardy had a heart attack some time ago, and that another like it might kill him!"

"As a fellow member of the board of Cipresso Wines Incorporated I have found your guardian to be a charming and communicative man. It would be a pity to have to dispel his fatherly illusions about his not so charming son."

"You are that embittered?" she said, beyond pitying him any more for his ravaged face, though it hurt to think of the little boy who had died in the fire.

"We all build dreams. It is a pity I must knock down yours in an effort to rebuild mine." His eyelids narrowed as he looked at her, his sun-dark skin was taut over facial bones it had taken generations to breed. "There will be compensations – Ravena."

Her eyelids had a pallid look as she closed her eyes against his use of her name. This day had begun like any other. She had cooked breakfast for Guardy and herself. He had read the paper and taken a wander round the garden. She had gone into the village for groceries, and on her way back had picked wild flowers and felt carefree in the mild sunshine.

She felt hard fingers close around her wrist and opened her eyes to find that Mark di Curzio had come close to her. The gloom of late afternoon had crept into the room, clouds brushed the treetops outside and the air smelled of rain.

Persephone, she thought, was plucking wild flowers when Aidoneus – lord of the dark – came and gripped her by the wrist and said she would be his!

She met his eyes, flinched from his scars, saw the flare to his nostrils and the suggestion of great passion about his mouth. All her life she had been fearless, and there was a quality of elusiveness about her that charmed some and disconcerted others. Right now she was at the mercy of her love for Guardy – defenceless.

"I will ask the marriage of Colonel Brenin. You will let him assume that you want the marriage as much as I do." Then he bent his dark head and kissed her cold, trembling hand, and as she stood there frozen she heard him murmur: "You wear trousers like a boy. You must understand that I want a woman."

He turned from her, took a flower from the nearby vase and broke the stem so he could thrust the flower into the buttonhole of his jacket. "I see you like flowers. Before the sun grows too fierce in Sardinia there are many flowers growing upon the hillsides. My home stands upon a great cliff of rock far above the sea – do you like the sea, *signorina*?"

"I have lived here most of my life," she replied, like an automaton. "I love the country around Ravenhall. I – I belong here!"

"Ah, but when a woman marries she expects to leave her home for her husband's." Ravena felt his penetrating eyes upon her. "This other man you spoke of – he lives locally?"

"Yes," she spoke blindly. "You can't expect me to give up all I love – *signore* – please – "

Then she looked at him and saw that he was not to be moved, and because to grovel and plead was not in her nature she swallowed her pleading and fell back on her pride. "If you force me to do this thing," she said, "I can promise to hate you with every drop of Celtic blood in me!"

"I have some Celtic blood myself, Ravena." His smile was quizzical. "My grandmother was Cornish, that is why I am called Mark. Do you know the legend of King Mark of Cornwall?"

"Of course." Ravena gazed straight into his eyes. "His wife loved the knight who brought her from Ireland, which she so loved, to be the bride of a man she could never love."

"Love has many meanings, *signorina*." He glanced towards the windows, darkening with the presage of coming rain – or summer storm. "The men of Sicily slap the face of their bride on the wedding day – we of Sardinia save the slap for the occasion that merits it. And now I think I will return to the inn where I am staying – the Wolf and Lamb in your old-world village, which has stables nearby. Being a Sard I was almost born in the saddle."

She walked with him across the garden-court to where he had left his hired mount. A black horse – steed of Aidoneus, who came for Persephone while she played among the flowers, carefree and happy.

He swung into the saddle with the suppleness of a man who loved to ride and who rode well. Dark Sard, who would take her away with him across the sea to his Sardinian household!

"Please ask Colonel Brenin to be available to see me tomorrow at noon," he said. "It is the polite and formal thing to ask a girl's parent or guardian for the marriage. You will also be here, to receive my ring."

Thunder growled, and horse and rider were etched darkly against the stormy dusk-light. "*Addio!*" He raised his hand and she watched as he rode away; the hooves of the horse carried on the stillness of storm, and then all that was left was the wild beating of her heart.

A sense of fatality gripped her. She couldn't tell Guardy what his son had done to Mark di Curzio. She couldn't hurt him, or risk another of those attacks that had laid him so low. "He worries about Rhodri," the doctor had said. "Our children are sometimes the love and bane of our lives."

Ravena thought of the four-year-old son of Mark di Curzio and a coldness seemed to grip her to the bone. The child's awful death had embittered the man to such an extent that he no longer felt the quality of mercy – least of all for a member of the Brenin family.

A Brenin must pay! She had been chosen because she could give him the bride-price of another child ... another son.

Ravena rose from the window recess and walked over to the dressing-table. Standing slim and tense in her leaf-green suit, she read again the telegram which had been handed to her downstairs at the reception.

It had been handed to her because at a wedding a telegram was assumed to be a message of goodwill to the bride. This one had been meant for her guardian!

It read: The prodigal returns, Da. Arriving three-thirty train. Love to you and Ravena!

Rhodri was on his way home! Ravena crushed the telegram in her hand and knew she had to get to him before he arrived in the midst of her departure for her honeymoon with Mark. She had to warn him to keep his secret, as she had kept it from Guardy. Dear Guardy, who had handed his sword to Mark so they could cut their wedding cake with it. Smiling, unaware that she was marrying Mark di Curzio to save his pride in Rhodri.

Rhodri would know that it was Mark's son he had

recklessly killed. He was a Celt and unexpected – he might blurt out the truth in front of his father.

Ravena snatched up her handbag and let herself out of her room. Sounds of laughter floated up from the hall below the gallery, and like a shadow Ravena made her way quickly to the narrow stairway at the other end of the gallery. It led down to a side door and in her urgency she forgot how angry her husband would be when he found his bride had vanished.

There was a slight mist of rain in the air as she stepped into the garden-court. No one saw her as she hastened to the garage and drove off in the mini-car.

The station was deserted as she drove into the yard, and filled with that peculiar silence of country junctions. The rail tracks were wet and shining as she paced along the platform; a bird perched on the back of one of the wooden benches and chirped knowingly.

The porter stirred in his cabin and glanced at his wristwatch, and Ravena tensed as with her nerves she felt the first vibration of the coming train.

Smoke drifted into the fine rain far up the track, and then the train came into view, following the curve of the track until with a rush it was filling the small station with its clamour. Doors banged, feet hurried, and Ravena stood quite still as the lean, dark, tanned young man came towards her, a holdall in hand, a suede jacket lined with sheepskin up about his throat against the chill the rain had brought with it.

Ravena shivered. Not until now had she realized how cold she felt – so cold, and she wanted so much to feel warm again.

Rhodri dropped the holdall to the platform and caught her in his arms. He stared down at her face for a long moment, then she felt the crush of his lips.

"Ravena, you've grown up!" He gave a shaky laugh. "You're quite something, little green-eyed witch."

Still she couldn't speak. She could only look at him, so real again after all the months they had been apart. She couldn't believe that this well-known face, this voice, belonged to someone who could be reckless and cowardly, drunk at the wheel of a car –

He stood away from her, the better to look at her, still holding her by the hands.

"You are looking smart!" He surveyed her leaf-green suit with appreciative eyes. "Nice after the sheepy girls of the forsaken outback. Where's Da?"

"Rhodri," she spoke his name breathlessly, "come to the car. I've got to talk to you –"

"Da's all right?" His eyes sharpened with anxiety. "He's not ill again?"

"No." She shook her head. "He's better than he's been for a long time. He has a part-time job with a wine company – a sort of director – and he's a member of the local council. You're looking well yourself, Rhodri."

There was no outward sign of a troubled conscience, and she supposed that eighteen months in Australia could have helped to blot out the memory of what had happened in Sardinia.

"I feel pretty fit." He picked up his holdall and held his other arm around her as they walked to the mini-car. "You look rather pale, Ravena. Your eyes are not smiling in the old way – something's wrong, isn't it?"

She didn't answer and they got into the car. She sat at the wheel and as she gripped it she felt him staring at her left hand. At the glistening gold band and the cool clear emerald side by side on her finger.

"Ravena!"

She turned to meet his shocked eyes. "I cabled to tell you I was getting married. We had no idea you were on your way home – "

"Married?"

"Let's drive and I – I'll tell you all about it."

The rain was like a mist in the air as she drove along the quiet country lanes and told him everything in a quiet, unemotional voice. He sat stunned beside her. Once he lit a cigarette, took a couple of puffs and then crushed it out as though he felt choked.

"You can't go through with it," he broke in. "I'll tell Da everything – "

"And kill him?" she said icily. "Don't you think you've done enough of that? A little boy died – "

"Ravena!" His face became a mask of pain and terrible regret. "I – I thought it could all be forgotten – the coward's way again!"

"We can ensure that Guardy isn't hurt – do you hear me, Rhodri?"

"But at what a price, Ravena!"

"My marriage?" She stopped the car on a quiet verge and turned to look at Rhodri. "I shall get used to living in a strange land."

"With a man you don't love?"

"Did I say I didn't love him?" The fingers of her right hand clenched over Mark's rings.

"You don't have to say it." Rhodri leaned forward and searched her face, taking in the shadows beneath her cheekbones, the determined set to her mouth, the proud, steady, cool green eyes. "I know you too well, Ravena. Your eyes don't freeze a person like ice when you're happy. They glow, Ravena! In the old days – "

"There can be no talk about the old days," she said. "You will say nothing to Guardy about what happened in Sardinia. It's over, done with, the little boy can't be brought back to life, and Mark will not say anything now – "

"Now he's got you to marry him? He must be quite a man to have got round you, Ravena. None of the Army chaps I brought to Ravenhall ever managed to charm you into a flirtation. You'd play tennis and dance with them, but that was as far as it went. They thought because you had red hair – " He caught at her with hands that were not gentle. "You little fool, Ravena! The marriage must be annulled before it goes any further. God, do you think I'll let you stay with a man who has forced you into marrying him? Do you think Da would let you if he knew the truth?"

"He must never know, Rhodri! His heart won't stand up to it. Ask Dr. Chaney!"

"As – as bad as that?" Rhodri's face seemed to age before her eyes. "You mean we're both trapped? I – I've got to go on with that kid on my conscience?"

"Did you think to escape without any punishment?" she asked. "Mark di Curzio is scarred inside and out. Scarred, Rhodri!"

And it was then that Rhodri Brenin broke down, sobbing dryly against her shoulder, like a boy. She stroked his dark hair and tried to soothe him.

"You must stay at the village inn until tomorrow," she murmured. "You can't go home to Guardy like this, and it will be better to go after Mark and I have left for Sardinia. Do you understand?"

He nodded and when he was outwardly calm again she started the car and drove on to the inn. But she didn't dare to leave him on his own. He was feeling desperate and for the present he needed her, and she stayed talking to him in the lounge of the Wolf and Lamb.

"Ravena, he'll kill you when you get back." Rhodri was pale under his tan.

She glanced at the clock on the wall and felt her heart gripped as if by cold fingers. For the first time she really thought of Mark and his anger.

"Yes, I must go back," she said. "Rhodri, I must have your promise that you'll say nothing to Guardy – it would be too much for him to bear."

His eyes were fixed upon her face. "What about you?"

"I shall be all right." She stood up, gathering together her handbag and her head scarf. "As everyone was saying today, Mark is quite a catch. He's a landowner and a big noise in Sardinia. I shall be the *padrona* of his house – "

"As if anything like that could matter to you!" Rhodri groaned. "You're the least selfish person I've ever known – "

"Don't make me out an angel." She managed a laugh. "By the way, Gwyneth Carew is still single and still as pretty as a Welsh song. Remember how well you always liked her? She was at my wedding today. She mentioned you and said what a shame it was you were not at the wedding – "

And it was then that Ravena ran from him, out of the lounge, out of the inn, into the night and the rain. She drove home to Ravenhall, her green eyes as frozen as the stone on her finger. She could bear anything now, she told herself, even Mark's anger.

She entered the house to find it empty of guests, only the flowers remained, drooping in their vases and shedding petals on the hall floor. A long shadow slanted across the half-lit hall as Ravena closed the front door. Mark stepped out from the library and she felt a thrust of fear as he came towards her, dark-suited, black-browed, anger in the hands that caught at her shoulders.

"Where have you been?" he demanded.

She stood silent and even as his fingers tightened on her shoulders she strove not to give way to her fear of him.

"Come, you will tell me." The very quietness with which he spoke was like the tip of a lash flickering over her skin. "You will explain your absence, which had to be covered up with a lie. Our guests had to be told that you were not feeling well and that our departure for the airport had been delayed. Deceit is something I dislike, Ravena!"

"Do you, Mark?" She looked at him and wondered what other name they could give their marriage. "You've heard of bridal jitters . . . I had them and felt I had to get away by myself for a while."

He jerked his cuff and glanced significantly at his wristwatch. "You have been gone several hours and I have the right to know where you have been."

"I've been driving around – " It was half true, but she couldn't meet his eyes and glanced across at the half open door of the library. "Where's Guardy?"

"He fell asleep in a chair, worn out with worrying about you!"

This touched a nerve and when she would have started across to the library, Mark caught at her wrist and pulled her back in front of him. "Have you been gone all this time with a man?" he demanded.

It had been inevitable that he guess part of the truth and she couldn't tell him the rest. She couldn't say that Rhodri was back in England and she had been driving around with him . . . he would guess that it was the

22

killer of his son whom she had talked of loving. She and Rhodri were not related, and to help protect him she had entered into a loveless marriage.

"Has the time come, *signore* husband, for you to administer a slap to the bride?" A cold despair seemed to give her the courage to defy him. "Did you find it humiliating to find your bride had vanished – that she was not waiting submissively for the honeymoon to begin?"

He stared down at her and she felt the warning grip of fingers that could have cracked her bones. "How much you have to learn about me," he taunted quietly. "Do you really imagine that I like only submissiveness in women?"

"You hardly look as though you enjoyed having to make thin excuses to our wedding guests, Mark. They must have – wondered."

"I expect they have been wondering about us for several weeks now. They must assume, Ravena, that you have married me for my money – what woman could love a face like mine?" His smile was a twist of the lip, and as he caught at her other arm and bent over her, she wanted to push away his scarred face. He must have read this in her eyes, for there was no gentleness in his touch as he bent her across his arm so that her hair lay like a wing of dark fire against the dark material of his sleeve.

"Yes, look well at my face," he murmured. "You will have to get used to it, *mia*, for I want no shadow marriage."

And then he kissed her, and it was the first time she had felt his lips on hers. Hard and possessive . . . a kiss without the promise of tenderness in it.

"You kiss like a statue," he mocked softly. "Let us hope that the warm sun of Sardinia will bring out the woman in you."

He let her go and walked away from her, towards the stairs. Then he turned to look at her and the kindness of a shadow masked his face. "We will stay the night at Ravenhall and leave tomorrow," he said. And then he laughed, quietly and cynically. "There is no need to look at me with such trapped eyes, *mia*. Our honeymoon begins in Sardinia, not here."

Her hands slowly unclenched as the meaning of his words sank slowly into her tired, spinning brain. "You mean –"

"We fly south tomorrow. Tonight you are rocking on your feet, and I am not quite the devil that I look."

Tiredness and a hint of tears blurred her eyes as she looked at him. If only she dared to tell him that she had been with Rhodri, but she was too afraid of his fury, too unsure of his mercy. "I – I must go to Guardy," she said, but when she reached the library door she had to look once more at Mark.

He leaned against the newel-post of the stairs, and there was about him a proud and solitary air, that of a man hurt beyond any more hurting. Hurt beyond any more loving.

As she hastened into the library her guardian stirred in his chair and opened his eyes. "My dear," he smiled, and held open his arms to her, and she ran into them, a child again, seeking the only comfort she was sure of.

"Mark was angry," he murmured, stroking her hair. "You can't run off any more, my dear, just when you feel like it. You're a married woman now, you know."

"Yes, Guardy." She pressed her cheek to his shoulder.

"You always were a fey one, weren't you? Are you sure you'll be happy with this man?"

She caught the note of care and doubt in Guardy's

voice, and at once it was essential that he be reassured. "Why else does a girl marry a man?" She made herself smile gallantly at the old soldier whom she loved and respected so much. Then she kissed his cheek. To-morrow Rhodri would come home to him and that would be her consolation as well as his, knowing they were together again.

CHAPTER TWO

THE mountain roads were narrow, winding in upon themselves like hairpins so that every so often the car seemed about to plunge off the road into the sea below.

Rain was blowing against the windscreen and this added to the sense of unreality and danger; of driving on the edge of nowhere to a destination that could never be real to Ravena.

She sat without speaking beside her husband and closed her eyes so as not to see the precarious bends of the upwinding road. It was as if the summer storm had followed them from England and would always be present in their lives.

"I am sorry your first sight of the island is spoilt by the rain." Mark spoke after a tense hour of silence, and Ravena opened her eyes and saw his profile outlined against the stormy light, the coin-etched side, unmarred by the marks of fire.

"Castel del Torre is one of the most scenically wild and beautiful parts of Sardinia when the sun shines and the lemon groves scent the air."

He spoke like a travel agent, she thought, trying to convince her that it needed only the sun to make her fall in love with his country.

Love this alien place, so far from her own home, so far from Guardy, who now had a housekeeper to look after him? She fought the homesickness that kept threatening to choke her and stared at Mark's hand upon the wheel of the car, burn scars etched deeply in the brown skin.

"You must be feeling tired." Mark's attention was firmly fixed upon the road ahead of them. "Another mile or so and you will have your first glimpse of the Casa Cipresso, the cypress trees will look like quenched torches in the rain, but the sun will shine tomorrow, perhaps. Below the Casa, on terraces reaching almost to the sea, are the lemon groves. Our vineyards are planted up the hillsides."

"Do you own a lot of land?" she asked politely.

"A fair amount." She felt he smiled in that wry way of his. "I am what is known here as a land baron. The people who work my land are the descendants of those who worked it for the di Curzios of long ago. Events do not change swiftly in Sardinia. Our way of life has a continuing pattern to it."

"You mean it's feudal," she said, and her fingers curled about her handbag and clenched the leather. "You're a kind of overlord whose word is law in these mountains. The people bow down to you."

"No Sard ever bowed down to anyone," he said curtly. "I have title to the land, but I don't take more than my share from the people who work it."

"They are not your honey-renders?" Ravena smiled to herself in a bittersweet way. "I see. Only your wife is the honey-render?"

"What are you talking about?" Mark cast a quick look at her.

"In the old days in Wales the *arglwydd* received the lion's share of everything – rending honey to the ruler in his golden house."

"So, Ravena, you will rend honey to the master of the house of cypress?"

"Yes, Mark," she laughed. "I shall rend my garments and my hair like a Sabine, for I'm nothing else, am I?"

"My people will call you their *padroncina* – little mistress."

She turned away from him and gazed blindly from the window beside her. He talked as if she were a happy, eager bride who couldn't wait to see her new home. He seemed not to care at all that she was lonely and afraid in a strange land with a man who neither loved her nor cared that she didn't love him.

Only love made you brave and eager to see new things, to meet and stand up to people who would be curious and possibly hostile.

She was the second bride to be brought to the house of the cypress, and her every instinct told her that Donata had been lovely as only a dark-haired, soft-eyed girl of the south could be. Lovely, and passionately loved.

The car turned a bend in the mountain road and it was then that lightning flared and etched in dark detail the towering cypress trees and the twin towers of Mark's home, growing out of the rock itself high above the sea.

It was like a dark brooding castle, and its cypress trees were like sentinels guarding it. The lightning flickered again as Mark brought the car to a halt and Ravena saw a flight of stone steps wide and foot-worn. And wrought-iron lanterns clamped against the walls beside the lofty front door.

The wind whipped her hair and her clothes as she got out of the car and stood at the foot of the stone steps. It seemed somehow suitable that she should arrive here in a storm, and as Mark joined her she saw the rain on his face and the lightning in his eyes.

28

"Welcome to your new home," he said, and before he could touch her Ravena ran up the steps and stood in the porch out of the rain. She was shivering with nerves and trying not to show it.

"The sunny south," she quipped, as Mark applied the great knocker to the door. "I can understand why you don't carry a key on your key-ring! Is everything king-size here at the Casa?"

Mark surveyed the great carved door set deep in the thick walls of the house. "Houses built this high have to bear the strong winds of the mistral and the sirocco. The towers were no doubt added to give the effect of a fortress to pirates landing on the beach below. In the old days a man's home was truly his castle, for he had to provide protection for his workers as well as his family."

She knew from the way he looked, the way he spoke, that he took pleasure in the strong old house in which generations of his family had lived and loved. All this was his heritage and he needed a son to work and plan for.

At that moment the lofty door was opened and to the echo of thunder Ravena walked into the great shadowy hall lit by flashes of lightning. It gleamed on the suits of Saracen armour, revealed the antique furniture, the vast, sombre-eyed portraits on the panelled walls. Walls that gleamed as bronze as the armour in the glow of the cypress logs burning in a great stone-work fireplace.

"A fire!" Ravena exclaimed with the relief of someone who felt cold, inside and out. She ran to kneel on the rough woolly rug and to hold her hands to the warmth in almost a supplicating attitude. The logs crackled, the only cheerful note in that great hall.

"So this is the bride?"

The words came suddenly from out of the shadows, and Ravena turned a startled head and saw that someone sat in a chair in a deep nook beside the fireplace. It was a high-backed chair with carving on the arms and legs, and the occupant was an elderly woman in a black dress, whose small feet rested on a footstool.

Her eyes were fixed upon Ravena, very dark and without a smile in them, taking in the pale young face, huge green eyes and red pennant of hair, damp and windblown from the storm outside.

"How young she looks!" The woman glanced at Mark and gave a sardonic smile. "Red hair but cool blood, from the way she crouches over the fire."

Ravena looked at Mark and saw the arrogance in his bearing as he stood in the firelight, a hand held out to her, his carved signet ring agleam against the scars she shrank from touching. She rose to her feet without his assistance and tried not to notice the way his mouth hardened.

"Let me introduce you to my grandmother," he said. "Donna Jocasta Leonardi, whom I call *la nonna* – when I am in the mood."

Ravena murmured a conventional greeting and wished she were meeting the Cornish grandmother of Mark. He had spoken about her with nostalgia, a Celt with whom Ravena would have had something in common. Though Donna Jocasta spoke excellent English, she did not look or sound friendly. No doubt she was thinking of the Sardinian bride her grandson had brought home six years ago.

Then he would have been smiling, his dark eyes alight as he called for wine and said they must drink a toast together.

"You will excuse me." Donna Jocasta rose to her feet, the dark silk of her dress rustling like dry leaves. "All day I have supervised the preparation of your rooms and the cleaning of the house. I am tired, Markos, and will have a light meal in my own room before retiring."

"To drink a glass of wine with us will not take long," he said, a quiet anger in his voice.

His grandmother looked at him, and then at Ravena, and there was a gleam of malice in her eyes as they rested on Ravena. "I am not so old that I forget how *lovers* like to be alone. I am sure your bride will prefer to have you all to herself, *mio*."

She reached up and touched his scarred cheek, her ringed hand lingered there as if she had second sight and had read in Ravena's eyes a reluctance to touch Mark, to be alone with him, to know herself at the mercy of his demands.

Ravena felt cold even in the warmth of the fire.

"*Buona notte*," the old lady said to her. "I hope you will find your room comfortable – the *camera sposi* is a big room, but none of the di Curzio brides ever minded that."

Mark escorted his grandmother to the foot of a vast, sombre staircase, and Ravena stood staring into the fire. The smoke of the logs was pleasantly pungent, and the soot on the stone burned and went out again, like fireflies in the dark. She started as she felt Mark's hands on her shoulders. He had rejoined her in that silent, panther way of his.

"You must not mind *la nonna*," he said. "She is elderly and fiercely Sardinian, and angry with me for taking a wife who is not one of us. Sardinians are clannish, you see, and very proud."

31

"It would seem, Mark," Ravena said quietly, "that by marrying me you have made three people unhappy."

He turned her to face him. His left hand travelled from her shoulder to her wrist in a single caress. "What makes you think I am unhappy?" he demanded. "Surely you know, Ravena, that I find you attractive with your red hair and your white skin, and your eyes that are the colour of the sea – and sorcery?"

She gazed up at him and her face was shut against him, like a mask. "Don't my feelings count at all?" she asked. "Am I just an object to you?"

"A pleasing one, *mia*." His teeth flashed against his dark, fire-burned skin. He turned from her. "Here is Renzio with our wine! We will drink a toast together and you will feel warmer with the wine of the south in your veins. Our own vintage, from the grapes that grow on the hillsides you will see from your window tomorrow."

He poured the wine from a Venetian flagon into a pair of stemmed glasses and handed one of them to her. The stem felt cool in her fingers, the wine was golden.

"*Saluta*." Mark raised his glass and added something in his own language.

Ravena looked at him gravely, tendrils of fire-dark hair clinging to her temples. "I'm not yet acquainted with the Sard language," she said coolly.

"I will teach you everything about the Sards." There was in his eyes a far deeper meaning as he held the rim of his wine glass to his lips. "Understanding, Ravena, was never won without a battle or two, that is my toast."

"Mine is this, Mark." She looked from him around the well-aged hall with its portraits of people strange

32

to her, its shadows and wrought-iron chandeliers, and great staircase leading to a latticed gallery. "I am not an actress with emotions written down for me to enact. I am here with you, but I feel nothing."

"Not even fear?" he taunted.

She glanced away from the staircase that led to the upper rooms, to the *camera sposi* – the bridal chamber – which she must share with him.

"There are stronger emotions than fear, Mark," she said. "There is hate."

"An intriguing emotion." He drank half his wine. "Your indifference would please me far less, *mia*."

At once she wanted to say that she was indifferent to him, but it wouldn't be true. She was unbearably aware of him in the firelight, tall, dark and arrogantly at home in this great house above the sea. There was even a certain grandeur about the man when the scarred side of his face was turned away from her.

"Drink your wine and give me an opinion of it." He watched as she sipped it, smiling, a devilish quirk to his black brow. "Do you find our wine to your taste?"

The wine seemed to have sunshine matured into it, elusively warming and imparting some of the spirit which had gone into it when the grapes were crushed. "I am sure your grapes and groves have been trained to yield of their best," she said. "A wife is a different matter."

"I am aware of that, Ravena." And as she looked at him she saw his fingers tighten on the stem of his wine glass and just when it seemed he would snap the stem of the valuable Venetian glass, he relaxed his grip and carried the wine to his lips. Each gesture had been deliberate. What he possessed and admired he was equally ready to crush. It wouldn't matter to him – all

33

feeling had been burned out of him with the death of his son.

"Finish your wine and we will go to our rooms. You will want to refresh yourself after that long drive, and before supper is served to us in the *salottino*." He gestured at a door they passed on their way to the staircase. There seemed to be many rooms and corridors leading to different parts of the house, but to Ravena it did not seem real that she was now the mistress of the *casa*. She felt a stranger who could never feel at home here.

"Our suite is situated in the Knight's Tower," Mark told her as they ascended to the gallery and he turned left into a corridor that led to a narrower flight of stairs. And as she walked beside him Ravena sensed that he had not lived with Donata in the Knight's Tower – they had shared the other one.

"What do you call the twin tower?" she asked.

"The Madonna Tower. They were so named by an ancestress of mine who was a romantic girl from Tuscany. Sards are not given to such romantic fancies, they are people of action."

There was a lancet window at the side of the tower steps and lightning flickered in, touching the edge of Ravena's nerves. Perhaps it was the combination of lightning and shadows and the unfamiliar that caused her to trip on the stairs and almost fall. Mark's hands caught and held her, and then suddenly his arms were around her, lifting her.

"No –" She struggled to escape.

"Be quiet, be still," he ordered. "Is it not the custom for a bride to be carried across the threshold of her new home?"

In one long stride he carried her into the *camera sposi*,

where lamps were lit, and where cypress logs crackled in the fireplace, casting a warm glow over the big room and its furnishings.

Mark stood holding her in his arms, close to his hard chest, inches from lips that looked as though they would be without mercy. "You look at me, *mia*," he said whimsically, "as if you had married Lucifer himself."

"I'm tired, Mark, and you are devilling me." Her lashes glinted as she half-closed her eyes to avoid his gaze. Yet still she could feel his eyes, admiring her hair and the whiteness of her skin against the dark fire of it. For the first time in her life she was really aware of how she looked to a man, and how helpless a man could make her feel.

Because that man was Mark she wanted to claw and hurt him. "I hate you," she said fiercely. "I hate this house, and this forsaken island you're so proud of! Stone built on stone, and you're more stony than anything else here!"

"Words!" he mocked. "Do you think mere words can hurt me?"

"Nothing can hurt stone – but stone," she threw back at him. "Nothing's colder than a cold wife."

"Such promises from such soft lips!" He touched them lightly with his own, brushing her cheek, the lobe of her ear and her throat. "But I didn't marry you for soft words and melting looks, or for tame submission. I want a child with all the spirit and joy in living that was in Dresti!"

And now she felt the pain in him, the hard tremor that shook him as he lowered her to her feet. He put her away from him and his face was a hard, scarred mask.

"The water for your bath has been brought." He

indicated the copper kettles on the washstand, and the screen by the fire with bath towels warming over the top of it. The edge of the screened bath could be seen. "Our amenities are a trifle Victorian, but you will be warm by the fire. *La nonna* should have arranged for you to have a young maid – most of our servants are men – but I am sure you can manage tonight?"

"I don't need a maid," Ravena said quietly. "You know we didn't have them at Ravenhall, and I am quite used to looking after myself."

"You are now at the Casa Cipresso and the situation has altered," he said crisply. "I shall tell Renzio to hire a young girl from the village. The *padroncina* is expected to have a personal maid. Someone to look after your clothes and to dress your hair."

"Doesn't my hair please you as it is, *padrone*?" She gave him a defiant look.

"You will wear it tonight as you wore it yesterday beneath your wedding veil, in a coronet. And you will wear the velvet dress in which I saw you when I came to dine at Ravenhall for the first time – you have brought it with you?"

As she met his imperious dark eyes she was tempted to say that along with everything else she loved she had left the dress behind in England, but someone had unpacked for her and before she could speak Mark stepped to the wardrobe and opened the tall carved doors. Her dresses had been arranged on hangers and there was a glimmer of silvery green velvet as he found the dress and lifted it out of the cavernous depths of the wardrobe.

There was a medieval quality about the dress with its tight-fitting bodice and sleeves and long full skirt. Ravena had bought the velvet a couple of years ago,

36

but had found no use for the lustrous stuff until she had seen a picture of the Lady Guinevere in a book and had found a clever Welsh dressmaker to copy the dress for her.

That Mark should admire and handle the dress, and insist that she wear it to eat supper with him, was a further invasion of her independence. She wanted to snatch the dress out of his hands . . . she wanted to be left alone.

"Very well," she said tiredly. "I'll wear the dress."

He laid it across the foot of the bed – the massive, carved marriage bed with four tall posts reaching to the ceiling and a coverlet of gorgeous Italian embroidery which Ravena might have admired at any other time.

Mark ran a lean hand over the carving of one of the bedposts. "Such workmanship is not seen these days," he said regretfully. "This suite of black jacaranda wood was brought long ago to the Casa by a roving ancestor of mine. See how the chests and chairs, and the bridal bed, are carved with all manner of tropical flowers and fruits?"

She watched him as he glanced round and took pleasure in the room. To her the dusky, looming furniture was awesome. Even the beauty of a tapestry of a unicorn among trees could not move her to anything but a sense of oppression.

"I am just next door," he indicated the adjoining door. "Please relax, Ravena. The Knight's Tower is not haunted."

It was not ghosts that she feared, and she saw Mark smile briefly and then look stern again, as if he guessed her thoughts. "I will leave you to get ready for our wedding supper," he said, and she stood staring at the adjoining door as it closed behind his tall, dark figure. So decisive was he, and so meaningful were his words, that his presence seemed to linger in her room. She was intensely aware of him as she went behind the screen and discarded her clothes and stepped into the bath she filled from the kettles. The warmth of the water and the log fire helped to take some of the nervous chill out of her bones, and when she closed her eyes it was almost possible – for a few yearning moments – to imagine herself back in the nursery at Ravenhall, when there had been a Nanny to care for Colonel Brenin's small son and the little elfin girl he had taken into his home and his heart.

Fleeting are the days of a happy childhood, too magical for more than a fleeting recall, and Ravena had to face again the reality of her marriage as she stepped from the fireside bath and wrapped herself in a huge warm towel.

The ends of her dark red hair dripped like a mermaid's on to her slim, pale shoulders, and she could see herself reflected in the gothic-framed mirror of the dressing-table. Something glinted against the dark jacaranda wood and drew her across to the dressing-table. A velvet case lay open there, to disclose an emerald pendant on a slender chain of diamonds, and Ravena stared at it as though at some sinister talisman.

A shiver ran through her and she drew the bath towel closer around her naked body, aware that Mark had entered while she took her bath behind the screen and placed the pendant on the toilet-table.

He had that right, to come and go in her bedroom as he pleased; to give her trinkets that meant no more than adornment for a body he desired. A young, vibrant, sensitive body that could give him a child. No love-gift, the flawless emerald on its slender diamond chain. It would match her ring, and the velvet dress, and team well with her red hair.

Adornment for the bride of Signor Mark di Curzio, who must have a maid, who must look the *padroncina* even though she felt a lost and lonely girl in a large, strange house.

She turned away from his gift and with cold hands she dressed herself and braided her long hair into a coronet. Once or twice she heard Mark moving about in the adjoining room, and her every nerve tautened and cried a protest when he knocked upon her door and strode into her room. He looked very erect and lithe in his dark evening wear; a man in complete command of the situation.

"Ah, you are almost ready!" His glance seemed to possess her from head to toe, taking in her white skin within the shadowy neckline of the velvet dress, the dark fire of her hair braided around the crown of her head, the mysterious slant of her sea-green eyes. She felt slightly faint as she saw the slumbrous look of admiration steal into his dark eyes.

He came to her and picked up the pendant from its velvet case. The emerald glinted in his fingers, and as always her heart seemed to recoil from the scars that marred his lean brown hands.

"Let me adjust this for you." He came behind her and she tensed as he clasped the pendant and chain about her throat. He gazed into the mirror, straight into her reflected eyes. "Do you like it, Ravena?"

"It's quite magnificent," she said in a cool voice. "A part of the family heirlooms, I take it?"

"You take it because I give it," he said meaningly. "There are ear-pendants to match, but you are too young for them at present. Your small ears are ornamental in themselves and will be spoilt by heavy jewellery."

His hands were warm on her waist as he turned her to face him. He gazed down at her for a long silent moment. "You are a sorceress, Ravena. Elusive and strangely lovely. I should like to have you painted as you look right now – all the di Curzio brides have their portrait painted in the first year of marriage. There is an innocence and a beguilement about a young bride that a man wishes to recapture as his marriage matures – yes I will have you painted, Ravena! I will commission Stelio Fabrizzi. He lives on the Costa Smeralda and can drive here daily for the sittings."

It was decided, and useless to protest that she didn't wish to sit still for hours while a voluble Italian painted her portrait. If she had to live here in Sardinia she wished to explore the cliffs and coves and the beach below the house. She wanted to swim . . . and she wanted to cry a little as she preceded Mark from the *camera sposi*.

A supper of quail, wine and fruit was served to them in the *salottino*, a room with a frescoed ceiling and curtains of tapestry surrounding deep window-seats. They sat at a long table, islanded with ornate silver, flowers in glass bowls, and the wine in prismatic flagons. Candles flickered in antique stands, and the carvings on chairs and furniture had a medieval fascination about them. Knights, panthers and dragons etched in the dark wood like steel engravings.

Ravena could hear the wind in the cypress trees beyond the long windows. The candle flames seemed to burn in the wine, and the candlelight was kind to her husband's scarred face, flattering to herself as she sat slim against the high back of her chair, the velvet of her dress a glimmering green against the carved wood.

The quail meat was white and tender, and Ravena found her appetite after a long day of tension and lack of hunger. A *pasta* in a rather delicious sauce was served with tiny marrows called *zucchini* and Ravena did not refuse the second glass of wine which Renzio poured for her. It warmed the body, dulled the mind a little, made acceptable for a while the strangeness of her surroundings.

Mark talked about the island and its history until they left the table and went to sit near the fire. "The evenings grow cold this high in the hills," he said, sitting dark against the damask of a great sofa while Ravena poured their coffee.

"I like a fire. It makes a room look cheerful." She handed him his cup and avoided a direct meeting with his eyes.

"*Grazie*." He gave to the word a kind of purring quality, and she felt his gaze upon her as she sat down in an armchair that matched the sofa, its damask a dark glowing red – the colour of wine and passion.

"Do you find this room cheerless?" he asked.

She glanced round and saw the candles still glimmering among the flowers, while overhead medieval lovers clasped hands in the ceiling frescoes and nymphs frolicked with satyrs. The room had a pagan quality about it, just as the man did who watched her, his dark head pillowed against the crimson damask.

"We might be living in another century," she said. "As if time had stood still here at the Casa Cipresso and the days of vendettas and duels and hunting with hawks still existed."

"Do you mind that?" His eyes flicked her hair and her dress. "You might belong to those days yourself. You have the medieval quality which is said to linger in certain faces – an element of sadness."

"Should I be smiling, Mark?" As she spoke she met his eyes, unfathomable in their darkness. He was too pagan to care about the feelings of his unwilling bride. The vendetta had only just begun for him and honour would not be satisfied until a Brenin had paid fully for Dresti's dying . . . for the memory of flame and unbearable pain.

Her gaze was drawn to the fire, to the flames breaking along the edges of the logs and gleaming on the great brass firedogs that held them. To think that escape from Mark had been within her grasp! Rhodri had written more than once from Australia, begging Guardy and herself to join him there because he missed them. But New South Wales had seemed like the ends of the earth and she had feared that the journey would be too tiring for Guardy . . .

"You are worrying about your guardian?"

She gave a nervous start . . . it was strange the way Mark could read her thoughts.

"I – I miss him," she said, pain in her voice.

"That is only natural."

"Oh, Mark!" A knife seemed to twist in her heart. "As if you care about my feelings! As if it worries you that I feel the wrench of parting from him! The only consolation is that Rhodri is with him . . ."

An acute silence followed her words. She looked at Mark and found his eyes glinting like dark points of steel in the firelight. "So Rhodri Brenin is at Ravenhall . . . it was Brenin you went to, straight from marrying me!" Mark leaned forward and pinned her with his

42

eyes. "You had to see him! You had to warn him to keep away from me!"

"Yes." She felt suddenly desperate. "He sent a telegram and I had to see him! I felt so afraid –"

"Afraid for his precious neck?" Mark's eyes were glittering, drawing her into them, drowning her. She jumped to her feet, in such a driven way that the full skirt of her dress swept too close to the fire. A tongue of flame leapt forward and the hem of her dress was smouldering before she realized the danger . . . then she gasped and cried out as the velvet was doused with water from a carafe beside the wine. Hands took hold of her and she was lifted savagely from her proximity to the fire.

"Little fool!" There was a marked pallor beneath Mark's sun-burned skin; his scars stood out lividly. "Are you so blinded by Rhodri Brenin that you can't see *anything*?"

His hands were bruising her, and the velvet skirt clung wet and spoiled to her body. She trembled and great tears filled her eyes, partly from fright, partly from fear. She saw nothing but the burned side of his face, the hell he had been through. The tears spilled from her eyes.

"*No*," she said, and it was a protest, not a plea. A crying out against the pain that had killed all tenderness and tolerance in him.

He let her go and turned his face away from her. "You had better go upstairs and take off that wet dress," he said. "I shall come up in a while."

She left him and made her way across the hall to the stairs. The suits of armour glimmered like ghosts, and she shivered coldly at the touch of the wet, scorched velvet. All she could think of, rather hysterically, was that

43

Mark wouldn't be able to have her painted in the dress after all. It would dry out, but the scorch marks had spoiled it.

It was a relief to reach her room in the tower and to strip off the dress. The bath and screen had been cleared away, the bed covers had been turned back and her night things laid in readiness on the embroidered coverlet. By the glow of the lamp and the softly burning fire she put on her nightdress and tied the sash of her robe. Far below the windows of her room she heard the thudding of the sea as it beat against the rocks.

The thudding seemed to keep time with her heart, and in a while she sank down on to a stool and sat staring into the last glow of the fire. This was her wedding night and she knew it would be useless to ask Mark for time to get used to him and his home ... she tautened when at last she heard him enter the adjoining room from the corridor.

As the seconds ticked by she played restlessly with the gold ring that felt so heavy. She heard the opening and closing of a cupboard. Something that sounded like a key-chain was dropped on to a table top. The bed creaked as if he sat down on the side of it to remove his shoes.

When the adjoining door opened suddenly and he stood in the aperture in a dark silk robe, Ravena couldn't rise from the stool. She could only gaze at him with her great eyes, her red hair tumbling to her shoulders, almost childlike in her long pale robe.

"You should not be sitting there with the fire almost out," he said. "Jump into bed!"

But she couldn't move and the room seemed to fill with his shadow as he came to her and lifted her from the stool. He carried her to the great bed and when he laid her on the coverlet and bent his dark face close to hers, she saw the anger still smouldering in his eyes.

He knew, now, that she had vanished from the reception to be with Rhodri. He would never forgive her for that!

"You little witch!" As he spoke he twisted her swathe of fiery hair around her white throat. She shivered uncontrollably, for Rhodri always called her "little witch". She closed her eyes against Mark's tortured face in the lamplight.

"Put out the lamp!" she wanted to cry out. "Put it out!"

There was silence and then a click ... it wasn't the lamp but the closing of the door behind Mark. He had left her alone, her red hair still twisted about her throat, the marks of tears on her face.

CHAPTER THREE

Dark night, sleepless and long, gave way at last to exhausted slumber. When Ravena awoke the sun was streaming into her bedroom, dispelling the shadows of last night and bringing warmth and the tang of wild herbs and the sea.

Ravena lay a moment in the great bridal bed, contemplating lazily the room that last night had seemed a prison. In the sunlight its splendours were less awesome; the jacaranda furniture had a dark brilliance to it, and the carvings of tropical fruits and flowers were exquisitely detailed. The unicorn tapestry glowed with colours and the seats of the stools were also in tapestry work.

Her gaze fell on the stool near the fireplace where she had sat waiting for Mark. He had lifted her as easily as if she had been a child . . . and then in anger, or because her childlike desolation had touched him, he had left her to weep a little, and to sleep alone in the *camera sposi*.

She rose and found a copper kettle of hot water on the washstand. She arranged the screen so that anyone entering the room would not see her as she washed in the enormous china bowl. These Victorian amenities were not strange to her. Her own home on the Welsh border had lacked quite a few luxuries, and apart from that she was not a girl to expect them.

Feeling fully awake now, she opened the wardrobe and inspected her clothes. She liked to feel free and easy during the daytime and selected to wear a jade-coloured blouse and a pair of tapered cream slacks. She brushed her hair and clipped it back in a big slide, and added a dash of lipstick to offset her paleness, caused no doubt by the tears and tension of her first night at the Casa Cipresso. She even felt rather hungry, she realized, as she made her way out of the room and down the winding tower steps.

There was no sign of Mark and she supposed he was already out and inspecting the groves and vineyards that surrounded the Casa. In fact she was beginning to wonder if the house was deserted when she saw Renzio crossing the hall in his spotless white jacket.

"*Buon giorno, padroncina!*" He was the perfect servant when in attendance upon Mark, but Ravena noticed a slackening of formality in his manner as he waited at the foot of the stairs, lounging a little against the newel-post, his gaze upon the slacks she wore.

"I should like breakfast, Renzio." She knew he understood English because Mark had told her at supper that Renzio, unlike most of the people on the estate, had worked abroad in hotels.

"The *padrone* is not yet back from his morning ride." An insinuating note crept into Renzio's voice. "The *padroncina* will wait, no, to join him on the sea-terrace where he always takes his *prima colazione*?"

"The sea-terrace?" A glint of eagerness came into her eyes. "I haven't seen it – will you show me the way?"

He bowed and led the way across the hall, along a side corridor and out through an archway into a billow of sunshine and sea-laden air. The terrace stretched away towards the blue sky, jutting above the sea, with only wrought-iron railings as a safeguard.

"The *padroncina* will wait for breakfast, after all?" Renzio murmured.

"Yes," she said, and she was already walking away

from him towards the end of the terrace, where she stood fascinated by the looming mountains, the far-down sea winking around the rocks that were grouped along the shore like ruined castles. From the sea-terrace one had the view of eagles ... it was no wonder that Mark liked to take his breakfast here, king of all he surveyed, master of the great house on its bastion of rock.

It was here that the bitterness had hardened in him after the death of Dresti. A man could not possess all this and be without a son to whom he could hand it on.

Ravena stood slim and remote at the edge of the parapet, the wind blowing her hair, an air about her of a captive bride of legend. She knew that soon Mark would join her and her nerves were tensed for the meeting after the drama of their parting last night. Her nerves signalled his approach even before she heard him stride out on to the stone paving of the terrace.

The atmosphere seemed to quicken, as with electricity, and she could feel her spine stiffening as he came and stood behind her. "Good morning," he said. "It has not taken you long to find my eyrie – tell me, what do you think of the Casa and its surroundings now the sun shines?"

"It's more pagan than anything I could have imagined." She felt the tumult of her pulses as she turned to face him and found him looking down at the sun on her hair. She had expected a cool and cutting politeness after last night, but he smiled, quirking a black eyebrow at her remark.

"The hideaway of a brigand who holds you to ransom, eh?" He took the hand that wore his rings and as he bent his dark head and brushed his lips across her hand she caught the tang of fresh air and lemons on his riding-clothes. He had been riding the groves where the

48

lemons ripened for crushing and bottling in the citrus factories further inland. The di Curzio trade-mark on citrus drinks was an established one – a panther crouched on a rock, lapping water from a stream.

"You had a *buon riposa*?" he inquired.

Behind his show of charm there lurked irony, and she could not meet his eyes as she replied that she had slept quite well.

"*Bene*." He turned from her as Renzio appeared on the terrace carrying a tray. Behind him came a lad carrying a large earthenware coffee pot. The contents of the tray were arranged on an ironwork table beside the wall of the sea-terrace, overhung by a great creeper studded with orange flowers. The lad with the coffee-pot stood staring at Ravena, for the sun on her hair turned it to a flame about her pale face and sea-green eyes with their slight tilt at the outer corners.

The girls of Castel del Torre were dark-haired with sun-warmed skins, and the boy had plainly never seen anyone who looked as Ravena did, standing against the iron railings of the parapet, almost too slender and young to be the bride of the big, dark *padrone* ... whose scarred face frightened the children of the village.

Renzio muttered angrily to the boy in the Sard dialect, and he at once put down the coffee-pot and hastened away as if scalded. The manservant gave an apologetic bow and held out a chair for Ravena. She came and sat down at the table, and somehow the staring boy had made her feel more of a stranger than ever.

"We can manage," Mark said to Renzio, and for the first time Ravena was glad to be left alone with her husband.

"You are strange to them at present." Mark poured their coffee, and the sun winked on the dish-covers and in the green gem of her ring as she added cream to the cups from the little earthenware jug. It swirled rich and thick on the dark coffee, and as Ravena sipped the delicious brew, Mark helped her to truffles and bacon, and a slice of crusty home-baked bread.

"They are strange to me," she said. "You can't imagine how I feel, Mark. Uprooted, half in a dream, hardly awake to the fact that this place is real and that our marriage actually took place."

He looked straight across at her, with eyes startlingly dark in the sunlight. "Eat your food, Ravena. Truffles – like love – lose something of their flavour when cold."

She felt a nervous contraction of the heart that he should speak of love. What did he mean by love? Holding her in his arms, possessing her but feeling none of the tenderness he had felt for Donata – girl of the south, lost to him as Dresti was lost, leaving him to try and rebuild on the ruins of his dreams?

She broke bread and buttered it, and found the truffles curiously flavoured. The bacon was crisp, as she liked it, and she tried not to think of breakfast in the secure company of Guardy, the well-known mountains of Wales beyond the windows of Ravenhall.

"Does your grandmother have breakfast in her own apartment?" Ravena asked.

"Yes. *La nonna* begins to feel her age and she is often restless at night and therefore tired in the morning. Sleep for her has become an elusive bedfellow, and Baptista, her maid-companion, often has the task of reading to her in the small hours." He gave Ravena a shrewd look as he poured more coffee for both of them. "You will find in the Sard character a toughness which you must not mistake for lack of sympathy. When *la nonna* becomes used to you and accepts the fact that you are my wife, you will find her less sardonic than she was upon your arrival."

"Is there a connection between being a Sard and being sardonic?" Ravena couldn't resist asking.

"You think I am full of bitter mockery?" He quirked that black eyebrow as he added cream to his coffee.

"Surely our marriage is proof of your bitterness?" she said.

"So I am bitter and you feel yourself the victim of it?"

"I know it was terrible for you, what you went through," her glance skimmed the left side of his face. "But it has made you cruel, Mark! It's cruel of you to expect me to behave as if I *want* to be here. As if it's only a matter of time before I adjust to being the wife of someone I – I love."

"I never asked for your love," he said, his eyes unfathomable.

"But what of me and what I want?" she demanded.

"If the man you want is Rhodri Brenin, then I think you are better off with me!" The words were as cutting as the knife he used to slice through the green rind of a melon. The fruit was pink and juicy and he glanced inquiringly at Ravena. "Will you try a slice? Our island melons are very tasty."

She shook her head and her fingers clenched on the edge of the table as he added sugar to his slice of melon and ate the fruit with a maddening air of calmness. *She* might as well be a melon for all he seemed to care about her as a woman!

"If you'll excuse me?" She bunched her napkin and threw it down beside her plate. She felt the flick of his eyes as she rose and went to the sea-terrace wall, where she stood staring at the mountains, blue-veiled, gold-spangled by the sun. The pagan beauty of the scene added, somehow, to her unhappiness. This place should not be sunlit, it should be dark – to match her despairing mood.

"Do our mountains remind you a little of Wales?" Mark inquired

"Nothing here reminds me of home."

"You carry the snow from your mountains in your voice, Ravena."

"And in my heart, Mark!" She swung round and stood in a defensive attitude against the terrace wall, the sun and wind in her hair, moving it like a flame "You've asked enough of me – don't ask me to love my prison."

"It will seem like that if you are going to rebel against the island – and me." He rose to his feet and came towards her, clad in knee-boots, his shirt and breeches a smoky-fawn colour. Lean and hard, with a certain grace of build that put Ravena so much in mind of a panther.

As he drew near to her and she saw the scars on his hands, she had to brace herself to bear his touch.

He took her by the chin and tipped back her face until she was forced to meet his eyes. "Do you think I married you out of bitterness alone? There is more to it than that, Ravena."

"Desire?" She put hate into the word.

"Yes, a little of that." His smile was mocking. "Also I find you interesting; a mixture of innocence and intrigue. Only you, Ravena, would have had the nerve to run away from me, and then return. You have spirit, and I don't believe in breaking the spirit of highly-strung fillies."

"Is that why you never carry a whip – because you don't need one?"

"Only the weak need a whip to tame a woman or a horse."

"Then you intend to tame me?"

"No." He shook his head and stroked the fiery hair back from her brow. "When we ride together, Ravena, you will perhaps have the answer to your question. When we are on the water in a storm together you will know me a little better. I don't like things that are tamed. I'm a Sard! I like the barbarity of our sun at high summer. The strength of the wind when it blows from the mountains, whipping the cypress trees, lashing the sea, shaking the olives in dark masses beneath the olive trees. I'm a Sard, my dear. We don't compromise with the elements, or expect tame submission from our women."

And as she looked at him Ravena knew why he had left her last night. The bundle of woe that she had been held no attraction for him. A man had to love a woman to woo her from tears to smiles and a need of him.

"Mark, let me go!" she begged suddenly.

With a smile that twisted the edge of his mouth he drew his hands away from her and lounged against the wrought-iron rail that was the only barrier to a plunge to the rocks below.

"I mean — " She looked at him with eyes that were the colour of the sea far below. "Mark, release me from this marriage — let me go home!"

"This is your home."

"We — we can get an annulment — Mark, *please*."

He turned to gaze down at the fret of the sea, and the unmarred side of his face was like a carving on a bronze coin. "Don't ask me for what I can't give you," he said. "Ask for clothes, for trinkets, for a garden you can plant with flowers. Ask for a horse of your own, and introductions to girls who will be pleased to become your friends. I won't deny you anything within reason ..."

"An annulment is within reason. We haven't – "

"We shall, Ravena." He faced her and she saw the glinting purpose in his eyes. "I take back none of the things I said to you the day I came to Ravenhall and told you about Dresti. I'll give you all the things a man of means can give a girl ... you will give me a child. *You*, Ravena. You with your pride and your fine eyes and your loyalty to the Brenins."

Loyalty ... loyalty. The distant thud of the sea seemed to beat the word into Ravena's brain. The seabirds seemed to cry it. Mark had only to use it and she felt helpless.

"A child should be born of love," she said. "As Dresti was."

"We won't talk about Dresti." He looked harsh and this made his scars seem more deeply etched. "I want to show you something of the estate. The sun is hot, so we had better find you a hat!"

They found one in the *grotta*, a flower room where there was a fish pond set round with wicker furniture, and cool green plants growing in tubs and cascading down the walls. Ravena gazed round the *grotta* that was shadowy and cool as a sanctuary. Here a person could relax to the peaceful sound of water trickling from the marble fountain in the centre of the pond.

"I like this room," she murmured.

"You may come here as often as you wish." Mark handed her a raffish straw hat, which she put on without the aid of a mirror, tucking her hair beneath it and jerking the brim down over her eyes.

"You are not vain of your appearance." There was an

54

odd note in Mark's voice as she bent to examine a plant with long green leaves.

"Vanity is an easily bruised peach," she rejoined. "Anyway, I'm not pretty. My cheekbones are too high, my eyes are like a cat's, and I never learned how to flirt."

"I am glad of that," Mark said quizzically. "A man with a devil in him can't afford to have a flirt for a wife. Come, let me show you the lemon terraces."

His hand was beneath her elbow and she brushed close to him as he opened a door in a walled courtyard and they stepped out into the sun that poured warm upon the descending ranks of lemon trees. There seemed to be thousands of them and the scent was sharp and dizzying. Grove upon grove, where men were working among them, examining the ripening fruit, or a tree that was not yielding its best.

Mark paused to speak to the men and to introduce his bride – and Ravena knew that he was tightening the bonds of their marriage. To these tough, swarthy, intent-eyed people she was the *padrone's* woman and an annulment would make him a lesser man than they thought him.

"I am a Sard," he had said with dignity and pride.

Ravena was beginning to realize that dignity meant a great deal to the people of Sardinia.

Sardinia, where the olive trees seemed to grow out of the rock itself. Where the barbaric sun drained the land of colour and etched shadows sharp and black. Where the fierceness of the land was in the faces of the people, and the scent of crushed herbs and cypress trees filled the air of the higher hills.

The stone houses of the *contadini* nuzzled the hillsides,

most of them with their own olive-yards, with flowers to offset the rather forbidding look of the olive trees.

Flocks of sheep roamed against the skyline, guarded by men in sheepskin cloaks, holding long biblical staves in one hand and looking curiously grave and lonely, like the Barbary fig-trees planted in the land long ago by the Saracen invaders.

The hilltop village was somehow Saracen-like, the houses pierced with narrow doors and windows, their roofs sloping all in one direction. There were shops like caverns of shadow, filled with tangy smells that came from sacks of beans and bundles of herbs; and a smithy where the iron glowed hot as a horse was shod.

Ravena strolled through the village with Mark and was shown the rustic old church with roughcast walls, a conical tower, and a nectarine-tree growing against its porch. And there in the centre of the village was the *fonta* to which the women had always taken their jugs until pipes had been laid so that water from the mountains could be pumped in their own yards.

Ravena glanced sideways at her husband and guessed that he had been instrumental in providing running water for the people of this high, stony village with its curious charm. Some of the women sat in their doorways and worked the small looms that always seemed a part of highland life. They inclined their heads as the *padrone* strolled by, and Ravena felt their eyes upon her slim, trouser-clad figure.

They reminded her of Donna Jocasta, who had hoped that Mark would take a Sardinian bride. More friendly were the eyes of old men who lazed in the sun in baggy trousers and sheepskin jackets, the smoke from their clay pipes mingling with the tangy air of the narrow, staired streets.

Ravena could not resist glancing into open doorways that showed a glimpse of austere furnishings and rafters hung with strings of onions and sausages. Hens grubbed about in the yards, and the brooding silence was due to the fact that most of the children were at their lessons in the village school.

"Their teacher, Signor Landolfo, dines sometimes at the Casa," said Mark as they paused to look at the small school.

It was at that moment that a small girl came running out of the schoolhouse and across the playground. She started to search for something on the ground, and Mark bent suddenly to pick up a scrap of a handkerchief that had fallen near the gate. He spoke to the child and held out the handkerchief. She stared at him dumbly, then she turned and fled back into the schoolhouse. Ravena saw his hand crush the small white square, then he laid it on top of the gate and they walked on.

"Don't be hurt, Mark," Ravena said quietly, and for the first time she fully realized how awful it was for him to see a child run in fright from his scarred face. She touched his arm, but he drew it away, not in anger but in a kind of resignation.

"It isn't the first time I have seen that particular look in a pair of eyes," he said. "Come, these old steps will take us down to the path that leads to the Casa."

The chirring of the cicadas seemed louder, the sun hotter, and as Ravena caught glimpses of the sea, she wanted to ask Mark if they could go right down to the shore and cool their feet in the water. But his silence chilled her, and she was glad when they at last reached the walled courtyard of the Casa and he said there was some paperwork awaiting him in his study.

"I daresay you can amuse yourself, or you may like to talk to my grandmother." He shot a glance at his wrist-watch. "About this time she has coffee in the *salottino*, and you must be feeling rather dry after that walk in the sun."

Ravena knew that sooner or later she must make friends with *la nonna* and she agreed to go and have a cup of coffee with her. She and Mark parted in the hall. He was walking away towards his study when she said impulsively: "You will have a cup of coffee yourself?"

He turned to look at her, a hand clenched over the doorknob of his study door. His brows were drawn like a visor, shadowing his eyes. "If there is one thing I don't want from you, it's pity," he said harshly. He pulled open the door and stepped into the book-lined room, and he shut the door on Ravena as if he wanted to be quite alone. As if she and not the child had hurt him.

She took off the grass hat, smoothed her hair and entered the *salottino*. Donna Jocasta was there, taking coffee and smoking a thin cigar.

"May I join you?" Ravena couldn't help staring at the cigar.

La nonna flicked ash with a nonchalant air. "There is always an extra cup for Markos. Where is he?"

"He has some paperwork to see to in the study."

"I suppose you have kept him from it with your sight-seeing? Come, pour your coffee! Don't stand half in, half out of the room."

"Mark wished me to see something of Castel del Torre," Ravena said defensively.

"Did he also suggest that you try and win me over?" *La nonna's* eyes through her cigar smoke were sardonic. "It will take more than a pair of green eyes to cast a spell over me."

"I haven't cast any spells." Ravena's eyes were pools of deep amazement, and then like a blow she realized that Mark's grandmother thought him infatuated with her. She had no idea that Ravena was in any way connected with the accident that had killed Dresti and disfigured her grandson.

Ravena's hand shook slightly as she poured her coffee. She was glad to sit down in an armchair, for her legs felt nerveless. Donna Jocasta disapproved of her because she was not an island girl; how deeper and more active would be her dislike if she knew the truth behind Mark's choice of a bride.

"Did you find anything to please you in our village?" *La nonna's* eyes were sharp as gimlets in their network of wrinkles. "When tourists come here they speak of local colour, of primitive charm, but they are soon glad to climb into their cars and to drive on to the Emerald Coast."

"I'm used to the countryside." Ravena sipped her coffee and tried to relax. "I enjoyed looking round the village and found it very interesting."

"You speak like a girl on a visit!" There was a malicious snap to the words. "From now on Castel del Torre will be your home. Here you will live when the sun scorches the walls of the Casa, and when the sirocco blows hot and dry and makes the nerves scream. And then when winter comes we are often cut off by heavy rains that make the roads dangerous. Markos will travel them, but he will not allow his wife to do so, and Casa Cipresso can be very lonely when he goes off on a business trip."

"I – I shall go with him!" Ravena spoke almost desperately. "When he goes to England he will take me . . . my people are there!"

59

"A Sard believes that a woman's place is in the home."

"Mark won't expect me to abide by such a rule!"

"What do you know of Mark after only a few days of being with him?" Donna Jocasta drew hard on her cigar. "I brought him up when his mother died at his birth. I saw him grow into a man ... the man you will never know. The man he was before the accident. All the best-looking girls were after him, and then he could have his choice of the loveliest, the one with the most spice and wild honey in her temperament."

The old *padrona* peered hard at Ravena, then she gestured at a carved cabinet that stood against the panelled wall of the room. "Go and open that second drawer. Inside you will find a leather picture frame – bring it to me."

Ravena did as she was told, she went to the cabinet, opened the second drawer and saw the frame, the folding kind with a pair of photographs set side by side. Without opening it she brought it to Donna Jocasta and held it out to her.

"Open it, look at it!"

Ravena obeyed with a fast beating heart, and just as she had expected the frame held two photographs, one of a bridal couple, the other of a man on his own.

She stared at the young man's face, lean and sculptured, and almost incredibly attractive. The dark eyes laughed, filled with light and an eagerness for life. The bold mouth quirked at one corner, and the quirk matched that of his left eyebrow ... Mark as he had been six years ago.

A Mark unknown to Ravena ... husband of the radiant girl with lace framing her dark hair and velvety dark eyes.

60

"Did you know that my grandson's first wife looked like that?" Donna Jocasta was enjoying herself. "In the Madonna Tower there is a portrait of Donata which was painted at the height of her beauty, when she and Markos were at their happiest. You must go and look at it. Donata was truly a gift from heaven for a man, and when heaven took her back she took most of his heart with her. When their child died, Markos knew that he would never love again, though he knew he had to live again."

Donna Jocasta stubbed her cigar in a brass ashtray and there was a curious significance about the way she did it. It was as if she emphasized the fact that love could not be rekindled in Mark.

"Please return the picture frame to the drawer," she requested. "It is a painful reminder for Markos, so I keep it hidden."

Ravena obeyed automatically, but the faces lingered in her mind, haunting her with their happiness. "I hoped we could be friends," she said, turning slowly to face *la nonna*. "But if you are going to resent me as a stranger –"

"You are a stranger." The retort was explicit. "You entered this house last night as if you came here against your will. Did you hope my grandson would live in England with you?" Donna Jocasta gave a scornful laugh. "You married a Sard whose roots are in his land, whose land is his life. He married again as he plants again when the harvest is over, because he needs a son!"

Ravena tautened against the carved cabinet as the dark, unfriendly eyes scanned her slim figure. "Mark's a fool," his grandmother grunted. "A robust island girl could have given him half a dozen sons . . . you look as if you never wanted a man to touch you!"

61

It was a dangerously perceptive remark. Donna Jocasta had seen a lot of life and she knew the sort of look a bride in love should have. She saw in Ravena only defensiveness ... a captive air ... as if her thoughts and longings were miles away.

"You are not happy?" snapped *la nonna*.

"Should I be?" Ravena began to walk towards the door. "You have just told me that I lack everything a wife should have. I am unloved, and I am unwelcome, yet unlike a stranger I can't pack my bag and walk out of this house."

She pulled open the door and hastened away from the *salottino*. She found the cool green flower-room almost by instinct and there she hid herself away among the screening plants, glad to be alone with the gold fish and the tinkling fountain.

She wished she might stay here and be forgotten, but at lunchtime Renzio found her and she had to join Mark and his grandmother for a rather silent meal.

When Donna Jocasta left them to go and take her siesta, Ravena learned from her husband that a wedding *festa* had been arranged for them by the people of the estate and it would take place that evening.

"This is always done when the *padrone* takes a wife." Mark lit a cheroot and lounged back in a chair. "You will enjoy the *festa*. The young men will dance the *tarantella* and the girls will wear their traditional costumes. One of them will be chosen to give you a gift."

"But, Mark," she bit her lip, and in her mind's eye she saw again the radiant face of Donata, "it isn't as though you had never been married before."

"All the same there will be a *festa*." His eyes and his

62

jaw hardened. "My people expect it. They work hard and upon occasion they play hard ... and you, Signora di Curzio, will look pleased and you will wear your prettiest dress."

"You may remember that you threw cold water all over it last night," she retorted.

"Yes, to save you from getting burned." His eyes gleamed dark as onyx. "I happen to know what it feels like, *mia*, to be burned."

"Mark," she at once looked contrite, "I – I'm sorry for being idiotic about the *festa*. I didn't expect it and –"

"And your conversation with *la nonna* has left you depressed." He leaned forward and scanned her face. She sat on a hassock, her arms about her knees, and she looked more than usually young and grave. "What did my grandmother say to you? Come, you will tell me."

"She – well, she said that when you go on business trips you will leave me behind at the Casa." Ravena's green eyes met and pleaded with his. "Mark, I have the right to –"

"To be with me?" he cut in, his eyes fixed upon her upraised face.

"To see Guardy ... when you go to England."

"I see." Mark leaned back slowly and lifted his cheroot to his lips. He drew on it and the smoke clouded his face. "I shall not be going to England for quite some time. My next trip takes me to Rome."

"Mark, you will let me come with you?" Ravena couldn't bear the thought of being alone in this strange house ... haunted as it was by the girl with lace over her dark hair, whose portrait hung in the Madonna Tower, who had been welcome here. "I'm used to roaming about on my own and I wouldn't be a nuisance. I'd keep out of the way when you have to meet people for business talks."

It seemed for ever before he said sardonically: "Of course I shall take you with me. If I leave you here alone, you may take it into your head to run away again."

The smoke of his cheroot drifted into the air and married with a ray of sunlight through the half-drawn shutters. His eyes were unfathomably dark, and his ravaged profile was in shadow, yet Ravena didn't find it easy to thank him for the promised trip to Rome. He wanted her with him so he could keep an eye on her. He didn't trust his own anger if she should take it into her head to run away from him a second time.

"Have you been often to Rome?" she asked quietly.

"Yes." He gazed past her and it seemed as if he looked into the past and saw places that held memories both sweet and bitter. "I spent my honeymoon there."

CHAPTER FOUR

No moon and a sweet, nearby scent of flowers. The stars were silent and lovely, and Ravena stood alone on the sea-terrace gathering the strength to be gay for the *festa*. Soon the *contadini* would come flocking into the courtyard below, the lanterns would be lit, and the concertinas would start to play.

Already in the big kitchen of the Casa food was being prepared for the feast, and this moment of solitude was a slender thread hung between peace and gaiety.

The full skirt of Ravena's dress rustled as she moved ... she had not dared to ask to whom the costume had belonged and had found it on her bed in the Knight's Tower. The skirt was of flowered frills alternating with frills of stiff silk. The bodice was richly embroidered and fastened with scarlet ribbons. A lacy scarf completed the ensemble, and somehow it had seemed appropriate to wear her hair in a thick plait around the crown of her head. She knew from the mirror in her room that the costume intensified the witchery of her eyes and the pointed charm of her face ... she waited nervously for the moment when Mark would see her.

The hot scents of the day had given way to a fresh-smelling breeze. The sea and the cypress trees rustled together, whispering secrets in the dark.

All would have been quite dark upon the terrace if it had not been for the small light burning in a wall niche in which stood a Madonna and Child. The steady little flame outlined the figures and revealed

Ravena by the parapet at the end of the terrace. She knew for whom the little light burned and it touched her heart, made pensive her face as she gazed at the stars.

Lamps of the angels ... she had come upon the description in a book and she recalled that she had read the book while curled up in a window-nook at Raven-hall.

How far away all the familiar places of her life, cut off by the high, lonely mountains of Sardinia, where all day the sheep-bells made music, and where the rustic churches added to the chorus at hours unfamiliar to her.

Mountains and leafy ravines in which lurked wild boar, and the occasional bandit. Lonely hillsides on which stood a solitary house of stone, and sometimes a conical *nuraghi*, the ancient fortresses of the chiefs of the island.

Time had somehow stood still here at Castel del Torre ... and Ravena's heart seemed to stand still as a footfall sounded on the stone paving of the terrace. With long, almost noiseless strides her husband came to her side, and he didn't speak as for a moment they shared the feeling of being suspended between heaven and the sea.

"There is no other place like this, on this side of the mountains or on the other side." Mark took her by the wrist and made her turn to let him look at her in the faint light burning for his small son. She, the wife of his vendetta, could not speak as his dark eyes travelled over her, and this time there was between them the significant silence of a tribute to the way she looked in the island costume.

"You look charming, but please smile." It was an

order despite the whimsical note in his voice. "The costume belonged to my grandmother ... I had an idea it would fit you, and suit you."

"Do you mean," Ravena gave him a look of amazement, "that *la nonna* is letting me wear it?"

"Not *la nonna*." His teeth glimmered against the dark bronze of his skin. "I refer to my Celtic grandmother. Demelza she was named, which is Cornish for 'thy sweetness'. With the costume she always wore this crucifix."

His fingers brushed the nape of Ravena's neck as he fastened the clasp of a gold chain with a cross of tiny pearls attached to it. The cross nestled against the bodice of the dress and Ravena touched it and found the pearls warm from Mark's hand.

"It's lovely," she murmured. "The cross of Demelza. Thank you, Mark, for letting me wear it tonight."

"I am giving it to you."

"But—"

He laid a finger across her lips. "It was never worn by anyone but Demelza. Girls of the island possess their own crucifixes, which are blessed by the priest. When Demelza came here as a bride, the cross of pearls was blessed and given to her by my grandfather. For a woman — and often a man — there is comfort in the possession of a crucifix."

"Mark —" Ravena felt tears burn suddenly at the back of her eyes. "Sometimes you can be — so kind."

"But more often I am cruel, eh?" His hands found her waist and almost spanned it. "I should like you to kiss me, Ravena."

She stood on tiptoe in Demelza's black slippers laced with scarlet ribbons and brushed her lips across Mark's unscarred cheek. At once she felt him go tense. He

67

knew she couldn't bear to touch his scars ... the thought of touching them made her shudder.

His hands gripped her waist, her head went back and her green eyes were wide open as he bent his dark face to hers and the stars went out. His lips were sea-cool against hers, and then suddenly his kiss was close, hard, and the coolness had gone. All that stood between them and the far-down thunder of the evening tide was the wrought-iron rail of the sea-terrace. A recklessness seemed to sweep over Mark ... it was as if he dared the elements to match his passion.

By degrees he broke the kiss, until his lips were at the side of her neck. "This should be a masked party, eh? If my face was covered –"

"Mark –" His name was bruised on her lips.

"My face frightens you, as it frightened that child at the school."

"No –"

"It does, *mia*, but like me, you will have to learn to live with it." He drew away from her and adjusted his tie. He wore a dark suit and a very white shirt. There was a distinction about him that was saturnine. "Come, we had better go down. Our people are arriving, the festivities are about to begin."

The great courtyard was filling with people. Some came on horseback, others in carts drawn by mules. The men looked like handsome brigands in their black and scarlet waistcoats and breeches, laughing, showing their splendid teeth. The women wore frilled blouses, embroidered boleros and long skirts belled out by several petticoats. The lanterns caught the gleam of their hoop earrings, and the curiosity in every eye when Mark appeared in the courtyard with his young bride.

"Welcome home, *padrone*," everyone cried. "Hullo, we are here to celebrate the happy marriage!"

One by one Ravena was introduced to a bewildering number of people. Her hand was squeezed, pumped and even kissed, and she felt the smile stiffening on her lips at the intent way the women looked at her. She knew they were comparing her to the other bride who had stood beside Mark – radiant, one of them, her lace scarf covering hair as dark as Mark's.

Her own red hair, her naturally pale skin, her inability to look relaxed, all were noticed. She wanted to weep to be put on show like this and was desperately glad when the ordeal was over and a cheer went up as the roasted veal was carried out on a great wooden platter, smoking from the oven, filling the air with a mouth-watering smell of herbs and rich gravy.

White-aproned servants followed with great twists of bread, mounds of *pasta*, olives, cheese, tomatoes and fruit. Giant straw flagons of red and white wine were opened and soon everyone was in possession of a glass of wine and toasts were being called out to the *padrone* and his bride. "*Saluta*. May the *Santa Madonna* bless you both!"

There was a curious hush, and then everyone drank and the moment of solemnity was lost in the feasting and the music.

Ravena was forced to sit beside Donna Jocasta and several of her friends. They asked endless questions, which *la nonna* translated for Ravena. She answered them as best she could and was glad when the music of the *tarantella* struck up.

The people formed a circle and in the centre young men danced to the swirling pipe-music, the lantern light in their dark eyes and their supple bodies full of the pagan grace of the south.

Ravena had never seen the dance before, and after a while she felt the insidious magic of it as more and more of the men leapt into the ring and the music grew faster, the excitement breathless, and girls began to call out the names of the young men they admired. A striking girl who stood near Ravena plucked the flower from her hair and tossed it to a dancer of particular skill. He caught it and put it between his white teeth, and soon flowers were raining from all directions, and there was laughter such as Ravena had never heard before. The laughter of people who worked hard, and played hard. In whose veins ran the hot sun, the wild wind, the rock and the harsh beauty of the land.

The *tarantella* came to an end and the men slaked their thirst with wine, and a guitar player sang a sentimental song. Ravena watched it all from beneath an arch of shadow, and saw Mark talking to some of his men, unbowed, never hiding his cruel disfigurement. The men with whom he spoke might have been the ones who had beaten out the flames ...

She shuddered, and drew back further into the shadows as Mark cast a searching look around the courtyard. He was looking for her and the lantern light showed how stern his expression was before one of the men said loudly: "*Padrone*, we must go out for swordfish when the time comes. Ah, that is sport, to harpoon one of those sea terrors!"

" 'Man is a hunter and he's got to find his prey,' " someone laughed.

"You speak of women, *compare*." The young quoter of the old proverb received a jovial thump on the back. "Women are the best sport of men because at heart they can never be tamed. What do you say, *padrone*, is not a tame woman like *pasta* without tomato sauce?"

"A woman whom a man doesn't have to fight with is valued less." Mark was staring at the arcade where Ravena had hidden herself, as if his night-dark eyes could penetrate its shadows. "Women are at the very heart of life, and when has life not been a battle?"

The men laughed and their vivid eyes sought the women in their colourful costumes. Proud, dark, with no hint of submissiveness in their manner.

A girl tossed her lace-covered head at an audacious whisper, and the next moment she flashed her teeth in a smile and drew her fingers down the lean cheek. "*Amante mio*," she murmured.

Ravena caught the thrill in the girl's voice, for the couple had found the shadows of her hiding place. She slipped past them unnoticed, into the lantern light, and at once Mark saw her and as he drew near to her the breath seemed to catch in her throat. He was so tall, so formidably dark, ensnaring her in a look that said in front of everyone that she was his.

"Are you enjoying yourself?" he asked, an ironic inflection in his voice. "As you can see, the men are now dancing with their wives and girls and it will seem strange if we don't join them."

He drew her in among the dancing couples and his arms enclosed her. It was a simple two-step, but she kept stumbling, and suddenly Mark's fingers were biting into her waist. "Do you hate my touch so much?" he whispered fiercely.

To all appearances his cheek was pressed to her lace-covered hair. To those who looked at them his whisper was that of a lover. Ravena closed her eyes to shut out the lanterns, the merriment in every face. "I'm trying,

Mark," she said, "to look the part of a happy bride. It's hardly my fault if my heart can't join in."

The dance music ended with a flourish and the moment had come for the *padroncina* to be given a token of good luck from these people who had flocked in from the hills and the farmsteads, curious, hopeful for the *padrone*, in sympathy with a man who had suffered tragedy and who was now rebuilding his life with a new young wife.

They clustered around the bridal couple, a young girl spoke a few shy words and transferred to Ravena's arms a most unusual gift – a spotted fawn with enormous eyes and long legs. Hers to rear and to make a pet of!

"Where did you get him?" Mark caressed the fawn's ears and flashed a smile from face to face.

"My sailor son brought him home from a trip. *Ecco*," a farmer bowed gallantly at Ravena, "your lady has about her a look of fables, *padrone*. The fawn should be hers."

"*Grazie!*" Ravena was touched, and as thrilled as a small girl by the fawn. He nestled against her, for all the world like a living toy. "Mark, please tell everyone how much I like my present!"

"They can see your pleasure, *mia*." His hand that had caressed the fawn touched her shoulder, warm through the silken blouse.

"*Mille grazie!*" She broke into the grave smile that put dents beneath her cheekbones and made her eyes glisten half with tears, half with shy willingness to be friends with these tough, kind Sards and their womenfolk.

They were indefatigable when it came to enjoying a *festa* and the merrymaking continued until well after midnight, when at last they began to climb into their mule carts and to mount their horses for the ride homewards.

"*Addio! Buona notte!*"

"*Buon festa!*"

The hoofbeats and the jingling of harness died away, the music of a concertino faded into the distance, one by one the lanterns were put out until only the *padrone* and his bride were left alone in the courtyard.

"The *bambino* fawn pleases you, eh?" Mark leaned against a cypress tree and his dark eyes studied intently the way she held the fawn in her arms – as if it were a baby.

"I've never owned anything so delightful," she said. "I'm trying to think of a suitable name for him – I rather like Bambo, if it doesn't sound too silly?"

"It sounds absurd." He laughed lazily. "Come, we must find a place for him to sleep – the stables, I think, where there is straw and where he can make friends with an orphan foal I have there."

The stables were at the rear of the Casa and warm from the horses and the bundles of hay. Bambo was bedded down, the cream and brown foal turning a lazy head to see the cause of the disturbance. He would have risen to his long and awkward legs, but Mark gentled him, the light from a hanging lantern revealing the scars on his hands as he urged the foal to lie down again.

How gentle those scarred hands could be! Ravena was shaken by her thoughts, and then Mark looked at her and saw her staring at the terrible marks, and he must have concluded that she was repelled by them. His black brows contracted as he rose from his haunches to tower over her in the narrow stall, with its tang of

73

horse and hay. His eyes looked into hers and their darkness was lit by shimmers of a disturbing passion . . . a horse stamped in its stall and her nerves tightened.

"Do you ride?" he asked abruptly.

"Y-yes, a little." His prosaic question took her by surprise.

"Tomorrow we will find you a suitable mount and you will ride with me. Tonight," he took a step towards her, "tonight you learn to live with this face of mine, and these hands whose touch seems to burn you."

And before she could move he swept her up in his arms and strode with her from the stables. His footfalls rang on the cobbles and shadow enclosed them as he carried her beneath an archway into the silent house.

Now they were quite alone. The party was over, and Ravena felt the deep beating of Mark's heart as he carried her up to the staircase into the deepening shadow. He seemed to be able to see the steps without looking at them, he seemed to know blindly every twist and turn of the way to the Knight's Tower. His arms were hard about her and there was no escape from them.

They came to a door and he thrust it open. The bedlamps inside had been lit and were burning softly, throwing their gold-shaded light on to the embroidered counterpane of the great bed. She was looking at the bed, at the two pillows set side by side, as Mark dropped her to her feet.

She swayed a little from the reaction of gaiety and the strong wine of the south, from being borne with unmistakable intention to the *camera sposi*. She clutched at one of the bedposts and her red coronet was tumbling undone, the lacy scarf curled down over her shoulder.

She stared at Mark and her eyes were filled with fear of the dark stranger who was her husband, who looked at her with dark eyes that smouldered.

"It was not in the bargain that we live separate lives," he said quietly. "You knew the terms before you married me and you must have guessed that I meant every word of them. I want a wife –"

"Because you must have a son." Her knuckles gleamed white against the black, carved bedpost. "Yes, I knew the terms, Mark, and I never hoped that you would amend them. I never expected that."

"You expected a lover?"

"Of course." She met his eyes gravely. "I'm not a child, Mark. I know that men can feel passion without feeling love."

"What man taught you to know that?" he demanded.

"A woman knows things she never has to learn." She let her hair right down and it fell to her heart, quickening as Mark took a step forward and gripped her wrist.

"Do you think I don't know that you refer to Rhodri Brenin, that you care for him – still?"

"How can I say I feel nothing?" Mark's fingers felt as if they might crush the bones of her wrist. "How do I forget the happy years?"

She looked at Mark and saw what Rhodri had done to him, but how could she deny the happiness of the childhood they had shared, their teenage years, and the officers' dances to which he had taken her, so resplendent in his uniform. Rhodri was weak, but Mark was too relentless in his own strength.

"We judge people from a personal angle," she said, knowing it to be true and unalterable. "You hate him, and I understand –"

"I fail to understand how you can *love* him." Mark's

face was white, and his angry eyes seemed to hold a look of pain. "Each time I look at you I see Brenin in your eyes. Each time we are alone he shares the room with us."

"Because you always have to mention him," she retaliated. "Mark, do you have to be so bitter? Do you think Rhodri hasn't suffered?"

"I expect he has a conscience. Did he return to England because it hounded him and because he hoped to drown the sounds of the crash in your arms?" Mark came even closer and the lamplight was full on his face. "Tonight you will forget him ... you will forget everyone but me."

She heard him and could not speak. The silence was utter as she stood there looking at him, into eyes like the moonless night that enclosed the house. The sea and the cypress trees were still, only her heart beat with quick strokes as she looked at Mark and saw with cruel clarity his handsome, ravaged face and the dark eyes burning with their deep fires and their deep pain.

She said something – was it his name? – then the ground was gone from under her feet as he swept her up in his arms and hid the scars of fire in the dark fire of her unbound hair ...

Was it really the truth when he said next day that the trouble at one of the citrus factories could not be settled without him? Ravena couldn't read his eyes. Even after waking to find him there beside her, her red hair bound about his throat, almost as if he loved her hair, she could not see beyond the darkness of his eyes.

He left before noon, and that evening a message came to say he would be away two or three days.

Ravena lowered her eyes so that Donna Jocasta – who was eating dinner with her in the *salottino* – would not see the relief that leapt into her eyes.

It would be a relief to relax from the continual tension of Mark's presence. She could explore ... the beach below the house looked wonderfully inviting. She had long been fond of the water and was a more than proficient swimmer, thanks to those enjoyable seaside holidays with Guardy – and Rhodri.

She tried to shut Rhodri from her thoughts, but he intruded in such a way that she knew he must be thinking about her. She sighed and felt Donna Jocasta glance sharply across the table.

"Do you miss him?"

Ravena glanced up and found Donna Jocasta's eyes fixed upon her. "Mark, do you mean?"

"Markos, yes! Who else would I mean – who else but your husband would you be thinking about?"

There was a sharp suspicion in the question, and Ravena knew that while Mark was away his grandmother would watch her every movement ... perhaps he had asked *la nonna* to keep an eye on her.

"I feel a little homesick, that's all," she said guardedly. "Everyone but Mark is still a stranger to me, and tomorrow I must get more acquainted with – with my new home."

Donna Jocasta frowned. "I have been running this household since Donata died. It will be some time before you will be ready to take the keys from me."

"I – I don't want the keys," Ravena assured her. "I'm happy to leave the running of the Casa in your hands. I don't want to upset things or change anything.'

"Why?" the old lady snapped. "Because you are not interested enough to try?"

It was a close shot near the truth, and Ravena was glad to turn and accept a helping of baked *frutta* with cream. After the meal she excused herself and said she had some letters to write. At last she had summoned enough nerve to write and tell Guardy that she was happy at the house of the cypress, and to describe the *festa* and the hilltop village.

She wrote also to Rhodri, and then screwed up the half-written letter and tossed it into the fireplace. No, there was nothing to add to what they had said to each other on her wedding day. He knew that Guardy's well-being depended on secrecy, and that if he confessed to being the reckless slayer of Mark's son, he might slay his own father.

She posted her letter in the village the following morning, and then made her way down the winding track to the seashore. Every now and again the path was shaded by a carob tree, or barred by an old bent fig or olive tree, and Ravena would pause to catch her breath and to gaze over the land that was harsh with rocks and sunburned *macchia*, and yet with its background of sky-capped mountains and dazzling sea had a beauty that could not be denied.

The stretch of beach below was curiously abandoned, and the sheep-bells and deeper toned bells of the goats added to the sense of isolation. It was as if the people of the hills rarely ventured to the sands. The dunes and the rippling surf were hers to enjoy on her own!

There was a dry rasping of *cigales* in the thickets of myrtle and juniper. There was lavender bleached almost white by the sun, and a wild sweet smell of thyme. Scents that clung to her limbs by the time she reached the beach, where she kicked off her sandals and ran into the surf for a cool paddle.

Mmmm, the water felt good after that long climb down to the shore, and as she wandered along she felt the seaweed curling about her toes and saw tiny crabs scuttling around the chunks of driftwood. She felt at peace . . . but it was shattered suddenly as a small, wet dog came bounding round the rocks, barking and scattering the sand as he came racing towards Ravena. Then he stood still, as surprised as she was, and changed his bark to a small growl.

"It's all right," she said. "I'm not afraid of you and you certainly have no need to be afraid of me."

The growling died away and the dog advanced with a tentative wag of his stumpy tail. He had the kind of coat that would be bushy when he wasn't wet, and a fringe of hair that fell halfway over his eyes. A rather comical-looking dog, the sort Ravena liked.

"Where did you come from?" she asked, holding out a friendly hand to him. This time he bounded to her and licked her hand, and his stump of a tail wagged furiously.

"Teo!" The call came from beyond the rocks, and then as Ravena glanced towards them a figure clambered over the barrier and leapt barefooted to the sands, a lean, dark man in levis and white shirt open all the way to his waist. He had sea-rough curly hair and the sun caught the medallion that glinted against his bare brown chest. His bold raking glance missed not a detail of Ravena's appearance . . . his gaze became intent as it dwelt on her hair, turned to flame by the sun and wind-loose on her shoulders.

"You have found a friend, eh, Teo?" The young man approached and his white teeth flashed in his bronzed face. *"Buon giorno, signorina.* How could a man know that he would be lucky enough this morning to find a mermaid on the beach?"

He added this remark in English, as if he knew who she was. But she could not remember seeing him at the *festa* the other night. He had the kind of looks that were not easily forgettable.

"I must introduce myself." He gave a slight bow and his eyes were amused. "I am Stelio Fabrizzi, you may or may not have heard of me – you see, *signora*, I am a painter."

His name registered at once, but Ravena felt teased – by his eyes – into a flippant reply. "You paint houses, *signore*? How interesting. I think the colour-washed houses of the Mediterranean are so unusual and they blend so well with the sunshine and the sea."

He laughed with good humour. "It was arrogant of me to assume that I am so well-known. You are the new bride and you also blend well with the sunshine and the sea – I thought you would be cool and fair and alarmingly efficient looking."

"I am sorry to disappoint you, Signor Fabrizzi," she said demurely.

"I am not disappointed, *signora*." His bold eyes held hers. "I consider it my good luck to find you so–paintable. All the di Curzio brides have their portrait painted by a well-known artist and when I heard that Mark di Curzio had remarried I decided to come and take a look at the bride."

"You were so sure that my husband would choose you to paint my portrait?" Bold as this man was, he was curiously easy to tease – unlike Mark. With Mark there was always that element of fear ... always the knowledge that he was as ruthless as he looked.

"Mark di Curzio is well-known as a man of discrimination, and as I have a small villa on the Emerald Coast it seemed almost inevitable that he would commission me to paint a portrait of his English bride."

"I am partly Welsh, *signore*."

Again his Latin eyes travelled over her, taking in her windblown hair, her sea-green eyes, her angular grace as she stood in the surf with the spindrift blowing behind her.

"Yes, there is a witchery about you," he said slowly. "It will be a pleasure to paint you, Signora di Curzio."

"You take it for granted Mark will commission you." She threw a piece of driftwood for Teo to chase and watched the black urchin of a dog go careering up the beach, scattering sand in his eagerness. She laughed and her red hair blew in the sea breeze.

"Maybe I shall not wait for your husband to ask the portrait of me." A touch of arrogance rang in the vibrant, foreign voice. "When I come upon a striking landscape I don't ask permission to paint it. When I see a beautiful woman –"

"I'm hardly that, *signore*," she broke in, and picking up the driftwood which Teo dropped at her feet she threw it once again and he scampered off happily to fetch it.

"Then let us say piquant." The smile in the Latin eyes grew even more interested, as if not often did the Italian painter meet women who were as lacking in vanity as Ravena. "What do you think of Sardegna, as we Italians call this island shaped like a sandal?"

"I find it unspoilt, even attractive in its craggy way. If I were a painter I expect I would find it irresistible," she replied.

"A bride should find it irresistible." Stelio Fabrizzi gave her a look that glinted with curiosity; a look that sent her in pursuit of her sandals, halfway up the beach. He fell into step beside her, a well-built man but not as tall as Mark, giving her for a moment the illusion of walking beside Rhodri. She glanced at him and found his eyes upon her, dark and yet with light in them.

"The toe of the sandal – does it pinch?" he drawled.

She didn't catch his meaning for a second, and then she realized that he referred in a subtle way to Sardinia and being the bride of a man like Mark. She tossed her long red hair behind her shoulder and her eyes took the sheen of green jewels as the sun caught them. The painter tensed as he looked at her.

"If you are asking me, *signore*, if I am comfortable at the Casa, then the answer is that it takes time for anyone to settle down in a strange country."

"You have beautiful eyes, *signora*," he said deliberately, "but I don't see any stars in them."

"In daylight, *signore*?" She gave him a scoffing look, and then found that Teo had run off with her left sandal. A chase ensued, all over the beach and around the dunes, and when her sandal was finally recovered, all three of them were in panting good spirits as they threw themselves down on the sand to recover their breath.

"Crazy mop of a dog!" Stelio rolled his mongrel pet in the sand. "He was a Roman scavenger, all dirt and teeth, when I found him. A couple of louts had tied a bone to his tail and it always hurt me – an orphan myself – to see another one tormented."

Teo licked the hand that had taken him out of the alleys of Rome and brought him to this paradise of sand and sea and regular meals. He lolled, cross-eyed with love, over the slim legs of the girl with the soft touch. It was a pleasant scene, the man and the girl resting against a sand dune, with a muff of a dog sharing his affection between them.

"You must share my lunch," Stelio said after a while. "I have a small boat moored beyond those rocks and a basket of food provided by my housekeeper. You will join me?"

Ravena's glance climbed the headland, to where a wing of the Casa jutted in the sunshine. Donna Jocasta would expect her to return for lunch in the cool, shadowy *salottino*, there to be questioned as to where she had been all the morning, and with whom. It was hardly an inviting prospect ... she wanted much more to stay here and eat *alfresco* with Stelio and his dog.

"Thank you," she said. "I am rather hungry and it's a long climb up to the Casa."

The painter gazed up at the house, its jalousies closed to keep out the noon sunshine, its sea-terrace jutting above the cliffs. It had a lonely, impregnable look, as if built to keep out strangers.

"Your husband will not mind if you share lunch with me?" Stelio murmured.

"Mark is away on business," she said matter-of-factly.

"I see. He leaves his bride to amuse herself, eh?"

"I don't mind," she said. "Mark can't let his business go to pot because of me."

"*Dio mio*!" Stelio made a clicking sound with his teeth. "If you had an Italian for a husband he would not leave you alone like this. He would be with you night and day."

"How claustrophobic," she quipped. "I'd feel like a prisoner!"

83

"A prisoner of love," said Stelio, and his Latin voice seemed to caress the words. "A man in love should be able to say 'If I had but the span of a flower I would share it with you.'"

"How poetical, Signor Fabrizzi, but hardly suitable for everyday living. I prefer a man to share his lunch with me – I'm starving!"

"How cool, how matter-of-fact," Stelio reproached her. "You say things that hardly match the flames in your hair and the jewels in your eyes."

"Poetry is wasted on a hungry woman, *signore*. Have you coffee in your lunch basket?"

"Let us go and see." He leapt to his feet and gave her a hand up. Teo barked excitedly, sensing that it was lunchtime, and they climbed over the rocks and came to a cove in which Stelio had moored a slender, painted boat with an outboard motor. He fetched out the food basket and beneath the shade of a carob-tree they ate a picnic of sausage and bread, herb-flavoured cheese, olives and slices of melon, all washed down with strong coffee from a flask. There was also water for Teo, and a tin saucer to pour it into, and after he had quenched his thirst he made short work of a cold chop and some slices of sausage.

Replete, they rested, and it was cool under the carob-tree with its great moist trunk and its long fruits. The sunshine beyond their pool of shade was hot and sensuous, mingling with the sea in a dazzling embrace. The rocks took odd, prehistoric shapes as Ravena gazed at them through half-closed eyes.

"You must let me paint you – Ravena."

Her eyes opened wide and she was alarmed for the first time with him, because he used her name and because she rather liked him using her name.

"Mark will have to be consulted about that, *signore*."
She stressed the *signore*. "He spoke of having my portrait
painted, but I'm not too keen on the idea."

"Why not?" Stelio leaned forward to scan her face.
"Are you afraid that a discerning artist will see things
in your eyes which will reveal you as a woman not
entirely happy?"

Her fingers stabbed into the soft sand and she
wanted to retort that she was perfectly happy, but
Stelio had covered her hand and was patting it. Bold
as he looked with his sea-rough hair, his open shirt and
his bold eyes, he was perceptive and kind in the way
of Italians. He understood that sadness was a part of
living and that in a way it made people more interesting
– to him as an artist.

"It is cooler out on the water," he said. "Let me take
you for a trip in my boat – after all, your husband is
away."

"And you think the mouse is entitled to play?" She
withdrew her hand from beneath his.

He laughed and his eyes were upon her dark red
hair. "You are no mouse, Ravena. You are like a Titian
painting, with eyes both vivid and shy. In every way
you are different from Donata."

"You knew her?" Ravena heard the quickened,
breathless note in her own voice, for each time someone
spoke of Donata she took on added shape as a person . . .
the woman Mark had loved.

"I met her with Mark di Curzio when they were in
Rome. They had not long been married, and it was
in Rome that her portrait was painted by a friend of
mine, at his studio. I met them there." Stelio didn't
take his eyes from Ravena's face. "She was an exquisite
creature, with immense black eyes and a mouth like a

flower. There was, my artist friend told me, no challenge to painting her. She was lovely and in love."

Ravena lowered her eyes, for she could see so clearly that radiance of Donata's.

"What – impression did Mark make on you?" she asked quietly. "At that time?"

"There was about the man a kind of Roman splendour," Stelio said deliberately. "I remember him sitting in Arno's studio, smoking a cheroot, his dark eyes lazy with contentment as he watched the finishing strokes being put to Donata's portrait. I remember thinking that he and his wife had everything a couple could wish for, beauty, health and love. There were no shadows in their eyes. No hint at all that day that he and Donata were marked out for tragedy."

"Don't – say any more!" Ravena jumped to her feet and brushed sand from her cotton dress. "Take me out in your boat – please."

They were out for several hours, for he took her to one of the small islands where there was a grotto through which a small boat could drift. The water-carved walls were of a curious limestone that gave off a blue-green luminosity and it was rather like being in a fairy cave. The water beneath the boat was so clear and blue that small fishes could be seen darting about like arrows.

"Here you should be painted," Stelio smiled. "Seated on a rock like a mermaid and humming a song."

"A Welsh lament, I suppose?" She dabbled her fingers in the water and felt a fish brush past like a slither of silk, but when she began to hum an old Celtic song the walls of the grotto made echoes that set Teo howling like a banshee.

Stelio burst out laughing and started the motor and

they emerged again into the open sea. Teo looked smug. He obviously thought himself a superb canine singer.

"You muff!" Ravena caught his head between her hands and gave him a playful shake. He thrust his cold, wet muzzle against her cheek and growled deep in his throat with that unquestioning love an animal feels quickly and rarely betrays.

The sun was setting as they purred towards the beach below the house of the cypress. A flame and violet sky overspread the sea, a tapestry woven of summer clouds and the sun bowing down to rest. As Ravena took heed of the beauty of the sunset, she realized how many hours she had been absent from the Casa.

"Tomorrow I should like to begin sketching you," Stelio called from the boat.

She stood on the shore, shaking her head and summoning a smile for him. "No, you must ask Mark's permission."

"Do you always bow down to your husband?" Stelio mocked.

At once the day went cold, a cloud veiled the dying sun, and Ravena was aware of the melancholy that comes with the end of a party. "Mark is not as you knew him in Rome," she said. "I think it would be diplomatic if you spoke to him first, Stelio."

The shadows deepened as Stelio gazed at her from the boat. "It will be as you say, Ravena. *Arrivederci*!"

"Good-bye – good-bye, Teo!"

Teo's bark echoed across the water and the sound of the motor died slowly away in the distance, Stelio in dark silhouette against the twilight sky. A last, rather sad bark and then all was quiet. A waiting quiet, for soon the tide would begin to stir and the rocks would suffer their ritual pounding. Ravena turned away for the sea was empty, and made for the stony path that had been cut in the cliffs to the headland.

By the time she reached the house, darkness had fallen and the lanterns by the courtyard door had been lit. She entered the house in the hope of avoiding Donna Jocasta, but the old lady was seated in her winged chair by the fireplace, her small feet propped on a footstool, her sharp eyes on the watch for the truant bride.

"Where have you been all day?" she demanded.

"On the beach." Ravena stood slim and half-defiant in the hall, her hair was sea-blown, her dress was creased and grains of sand clung to her limbs. She looked very young, half on the verge of flight. But to flee up the stairs would make her look guilty, and she felt no guilt about the hours she had spent in the company of Stelio Fabrizzi. He had helped with his charm to alleviate her homesickness and she was grateful to him.

"Baptista saw you with a man! I sent her to scan the beach from the sea-terrace and fluttery spinster that she is, she knows a man when she sees one. Well, what have you to say?"

"That Baptista has excellent eyesight." Ravena's defiance had found its way into her voice. "I met a friend of Mark's down on the beach. A Signor Fabrizzi."

Donna Jocasta drew in her breath. "That artist?"

"Yes."

"All artists are gay and wicked, and you have been with him all day?"

"Most of the day, with his dog." Ravena began to

make for the stairs. "I'm grubby and would like to have a bath."

"One moment!"

Ravena turned obediently, a hand clenching the carved newel-post.

"You will see no more of this man. I forbid it!"

"I'm not a child, Donna Jocasta." Anger shook in Ravena's voice. "You can't forbid me a friendship, or act the dragon because Mark is away for a few days. I – I won't put up with it!"

"Markos left you in my charge –"

"Did he say you were to lock me in the tower, and to keep me on bread and water?" Ravena threw back her head and her sea-bloomed hair gave a crackle. "Well, I don't intend to be shut up in this dark old house. Tomorrow I shall go again to the beach and I hope Signor Fabrizzi is there. He laughs, *signora*. He's full of life and he looks to the future and doesn't dwell in the past all the time."

Ravena swung round and raced up the stairs and along the gallery to the narrow stairway to the Knight's Tower. Her cheeks were hot, her heart was pounding, and she felt that she hated Mark for leaving orders that she be spied upon. She hated this house and would spend all day tomorrow out in the sun and wind – with Stelio.

CHAPTER FIVE

RAVENA's day on the beach had tired her out and she awoke the following morning to find the sunshine so bright in her room that she knew at once that she had overslept.

She sat up and found a covered tray on the bedside table. She settled it across her knees and poured coffee from the little silver pot, and enjoyed the ham and eggs with appetite. The day was hers again, to do just as she liked. Donna Jocasta could not keep her locked in her room!

Half an hour later she was washed and dressed and at the mirror fixing her hair in a pony-tail. It combined with her shirt and trews to make her look very young, and a thoughtful look came into her eyes as she gazed at her reflection. She felt a stirring of curiosity about the portrait of Donata that hung in the Madonna Tower; she recalled what Stelio Fabrizzi had said about Mark when he had met him in Rome six years ago. He had been splendid and happy ... there had been no shadows in his eyes.

She wanted to see the portrait, right now, before she went down to the beach, and she hurried to her bedroom door and opened it. There was no one about. The servants would be busy dusting and polishing in the rooms below. These upper rooms would not receive attention until later, which meant she could cross to the Madonna Tower unobserved.

She let herself out of the Knight's Tower by a door

set deep in the wall, and was confronted by the narrow stone bridge that soared between the twin towers, joining them together.

Far below were the courtyards, and the descending ranks of lemon trees, drinking in the sunshine and scenting the air. Birds hovered about the battlements of the towers, along which signal fires had flared long ago, to give warning of pirates or some other enemy. This island had attracted many strangers, yet like the Welsh the people remained strongly, firmly individual.

Ravena stood in the centre of the bridge and felt the wind in her hair. She was struck by her own response to this place . . . as a visitor she could have enjoyed herself immensely.

The Madonna Tower was like its twin in every respect. A door set deep in the wall led into a dim corridor, lit by a narrow window, and the apartment in which Mark had lived with Donata was almost a replica of the *camera sposi* he now occupied with Ravena.

An ornate bedroom with a gloom of its own. The secrets of long ago were locked in its panels and carvings. Its long brocade curtains held whispers, its deep carpet was quiet as smoke to walk across, and there on the wall hung the portrait of the girl to whom Mark had been devoted.

In the dimness of the room Ravena couldn't make out the features or the dress of Mark's first wife. Candlesticks stood below on the mantelpiece and there beside the candles were matches, as if someone came now and then to light up the portrait and to study it in the whispering stillness of the big room.

Ravena struck a match and lit the candles, which sputtered and smoked and cast their flickering light upwards. She saw a dress copied from the Medici times, falling in graceful folds of Madonna-blue about the slender figure of Donata. Pearls were entwined in her dark, glossy hair, and more pearls in intricate settings hung about her long, creamy throat. So lovely she was a pleasure and a pain to look at.

Ravena lost sense of time as she held a candlestick and gazed at the girl who had given so much joy to Mark that no other woman could ever replace her image in his heart, his mind and his senses. She looked very young . . . Mark himself would have been in his twenties when they were married.

Donata . . . gift from heaven.

A sigh stole from Ravena's lips and still holding the candlestick she turned from the portrait and felt the painted eyes upon her as she gazed around the room in which Donata had slept and loved and wandered about in lovely things like the Medici gown she wore in the portrait.

The candle flame made flickering shadows on the panelling of the walls. It struck Ravena as strange, and yet at the same time as inevitable, that no white sheets swathed the furniture of Donata's bedroom. To cover furniture was to turn it into so many ghosts. To hide the brushes and combs and scent-bottles she had used was to make positive the fact that she was no more than a memory.

Ravena breathed the scent of flowers and found upon following the scent that outside the windows hung a golden mass of honeysuckle. She held back the brocade curtain and saw that the windows were open a few inches to air the room and let in the scent which Donata must have loved.

She let the curtain fall into place again and her eyes

sought the small clock that stood on the antique table beside the great bed, canopied in chintz like the bed of a queen, but the hands were still, there was no ticking to disturb the silence. Time stood still in the Madonna Tower, each article on the toilet-table was as Donata had left it; the flower that had fallen into papery flakes might have been a flower she had worn in her hair ... perhaps Mark had plucked it for her.

On impulse Ravena opened the enormous wardrobe that reached almost to the ceiling, and because everything else was untouched it came as a slight shock that the wardrobe was empty. All it contained was a musty scent; gone were the velvets and silks and cobweb-lace Donata would have worn.

Perhaps it had been too poignant for Mark to see the clothes in which his wife had looked so regal and radiant. Perhaps, in an excess of grief, he had given orders that they be given away.

Ravena closed the wardrobe doors and as she turned again to face the room, her eyes met those of the portrait, and for a chilling moment they seemed alive and aware ... and antagonistic. Ravena drew in her breath and at the same time a draught fluttered the candle flame and blew it out. At once there were shadows, made long and sinister by that single candle burning on the mantelpiece, and in a panic Ravena ran to the door and wrenched at the handle. It turned impotently, from side to side ... the door wouldn't budge, and when she ran into the adjoining room and tried the door that led into the corridor, that too was firmly shut ... locked.

For a stunned moment she could hardly take in the incredible fact that she was locked in the tower apartment ... that someone had crept along the corridor and locked both doors, knowing she was in here, alone with the portrait.

Anger swept her and she thumped on the door with her fist. Again, and yet again, until she realized the futility of the action. She had been locked into these rooms for one of two reasons, either to punish her for yesterday . . . or to frighten her.

She turned and stood with her back to the door, and then she hastened to the nearest window and jerked the curtain aside. There was dust in the material. This room, which must have been the bedroom occupied by Mark, was not kept as aired or dust-free as the adjoining room, and the dust made Ravena sneeze as she pushed open the window and leaned out. There was a well of distance from the tower to the courtyard below, and as she hung out of the window, her distressed eyes and her long hair gave her the look of a captive maiden of long ago, locked in the tower and searching for a way of escape . . . or for a gallant rescuer.

There was no one. The courtyard was empty, and the workers in the lemon groves were hidden from sight by the trees. The wind blew around the tower and the cries of birds were like a plaintive mockery. They had wings and could fly away if they wished . . . she was trapped in here until someone came to let her out.

It was Donna Jocasta who had locked her in, or sent the obedient Baptista to do so. She was no more than a dark shadow who followed in her mistress's wake, too old now to find other employment and afraid to disobey the eccentric orders that came her way.

A cold tremor ran through Ravena. There was no telling what time it was, and it might be hours before Donna Jocasta let her out of the tower. A salutary lesson for Mark's bride, because she dared to talk to another man and had said defiantly that she meant to see him again!

She gazed around at the panelled walls and wondered if one of them concealed a secret stairway. Surely it was possible? Long ago, at the time of the pirate raids and the Saracen invasions, a man would not have built a house without secret chambers where his family could be concealed, or a stairway down which they could escape if the invaders got into the house.

Ravena set about thumping the panels and testing each likely-looking piece of carving, but nothing yielded to her touch, no dark panel swung open to reveal narrow twisting stairs set inside the thick walls.

With some reluctance she entered the room of the portrait and tried the panels in there, but if there was a concealed compartment it was well hidden.

She wiped her dusty hands on her trews and once again her eyes were caught and held by those of the portrait. The candle had burned lower, shadowing the painted face so that only the eyes held light in them. The effect was disturbing, for Donata's smile was on her flower-like mouth, not in her eyes. They were the eyes of someone who relished her own beauty and the power it gave her over those who loved her. They were brilliant with self-awareness ... in the Medici gown and the di Curzio pearls, Donata had known herself beyond compare.

Ravena turned away from the portrait and caught sight of herself in the mirror of the dressing-table. She stared at her pony-tailed hair, her dusty trews and boyish shirt, and found it hard to believe that she was Mark's wife. It seemed to her that Donata still reigned here as mistress; that the girl reflected in the mirror was no more than the naughty child she looked.

"You dress like a boy," Mark had said to her that fateful day at Ravenhall. "I expect to marry a woman."

She fingered the gold ring that signified their marriage, and without glancing again at Donata's portrait she wandered back into the room which had been Mark's. Beneath the window where she had dragged open the curtain was a deep recess and she curled down in it, looking and feeling like a disconsolate cat. The sky beyond was a hot blue and the cypress trees were etched dark and towering against the blueness.

It was a beautiful morning, yet here she was shut up in the tower like a damsel in a Grimm fairy-tale!

It was so ludicrous that she laughed. At the same time it was beyond a joke that she should be robbed in this way of the sunny hours she had meant to spend with Stelio Fabrizzi and his dog Teo. He would have guessed long since that she wasn't free to join him on the beach for a picnic and he would have chugged off in his boat. Free as a bird himself, he would not have dreamed that she was locked up like this.

She thought of Guardy, who would believe her happy when he received her letter. Happiness? How was she to ever find it in this house, haunted as it was by the young and forever lovely Donata; ruled as it was by the elderly woman who had wanted her grandson to marry a girl of her choosing.

Ravena's heart felt weighted down by the silence and the solitude, and by the sudden fear that Mark would be away for days and she would be left at the mercy of further eccentricities. Further tricks to undermine her spirit and make of her another obedient shadow like Baptista.

"*No!*" she gasped, and ran to the door to see if it would open. It wouldn't, and she slumped against the

96

panels and felt like crying. She swallowed the lump that came into her throat and consoled herself with the thought that Donna Jocasta would let her out when lunchtime came. She wouldn't be so cruel as to leave her here until darkness began to fall and the owls began to hoot in the trees, and the shadows stalked closer.

She took a cushion from a chair, thumped the dust out of it and made herself as comfortable as possible in the window recess. She would close her eyes and pretend she was back at Ravenhall ... yes, there was the old elm tree and the rockery, and the swing from which she had fallen that time Rhodri had swung her too high. Up and up, into the boughs of a tree laden with spring-time blossom. It was delicious to fly so high, and fearful.

"*No!*" she gasped laughingly, but he took no notice of her alarm and went on pushing the swing, until she was among the blossom and lost in it, and then with a jolt was out of the swing and falling.

"Ravena!"

She stirred and felt the pain in her arm. "Oh, Rhodri – "

The hand on her hair withdrew sharply and she awoke fully with a startled cry and saw that it was Mark who was bending over her, and that her shoulder hurt because it had been pressing against the edge of the window recess.

"Mark!"

"I am sorry to disturb your pleasant dreams," he said.

She sat up and rubbed her numbed arm, and felt a little dazed. "I – I fell asleep," she said bemusedly.

"What are you doing in here?" he demanded.

She felt his eyes rake her dishevelled hair and her

boyish garb, and suddenly she felt so cold. "Someone locked me in here – hours ago!" she blurted. "It was your grandmother, Mark. I know it was!"

"Locked you in?" He frowned and gestured at the door, which stood wide open from his own entrance into the room. "The door was not locked, as you can see, and why you should imagine my grandmother would do such a thing is beyond me."

"I'm not imagining it!" He made her feel helpless and unsure, towering over her, and she jumped to her feet. "Donna Jocasta dislikes me – she wanted to frighten me!"

His dark face expressed surprise and disbelief. "I suppose you came to these rooms out of curiosity? They are no longer in use and the locks grow stiff – "

"I was locked in, Mark. I thumped and banged on this door and the one in the other room, but neither of them would open."

"Where is the key?" He gestured once again at the door with its empty lock.

"Donna Jocasta has all the keys of the house. She told me so the other evening, that all the keys of the Casa were in her keeping and that she was not handing them over to me."

"Did you ask for them?"

"Of course not." Ravena sighed and pushed the red hair back off her forehead. "It wasn't over the running of the Casa that we quarrelled."

"You will tell me what it was over!"

"I went down to the beach yesterday and meant to go again today." Ravena tilted her chin and met her husband's dark, forbidding eyes. "I met Stelio Fabrizzi down on the beach and he took me out in his boat to a grotto on one of the little islands. When I returned home, your grandmother demanded to know where I had been, and when I told her, she forbade me to see Signor Fabrizzi again. I thought she was being dictatorial and I told her so. I said she couldn't forbid me to make my own friends. This morning she must have seen me crossing the bridge to the Madonna Tower, and I'm quite certain she ordered Baptista to lock me in, so I wouldn't be able to go to the beach."

"You arranged to see Fabrizzi today?"

The question struck like a lash, reminding Ravena that it was her husband to whom she was talking and that he might object even more strongly to her friendship with the attractive artist.

"We made a tentative arrangement," she admitted, and the fast beating of her heart made her voice shake slightly. "He said he wanted to sketch me. I – I said he should ask you."

"I am gratified that you remembered my existence at all." Mark took her by the wrist and the grim set to his lips seemed to relax slightly. "I should not be angry with you. You are new to our ways and regard everything as a curb on your freedom."

"I should think being locked in a tower is a curb on a girl's freedom!"

"*La nonna* is very much a Sard and she probably thought she was doing her best to safeguard you."

"Mark, I ate sausage and cheese with Signor Fabrizzi and played chase with his dog. For that I am treated like a child who has misbehaved."

"You are not a child in my grandmother's eyes. You are a woman – my wife – who met alone with a man. To the people of this island a man and woman meet alone for only one purpose, and that is to make love."

"Mark – it's absurd! In my country men and women

can be friends without being – lovers."

"This is now your country, Ravena."

An involuntary tremor ran through her and Mark must have felt it, for his grip tightened, bringing her closer to him, and to look into his eyes was to be drowned in them.

"Need I add that I have the right to be the only man in your thoughts." His hand enclosed her throat, caressingly, and he tipped back her head until her hair was a red rain in the shaft of sunlight through the window. "Did you come to look at the portrait in the other room?" he murmured. "Were you curious to see if Donata was lovelier, warmer, more womanly than yourself?"

And then, as if in hunger for all he had lost, he crushed Ravena's lips beneath his and his fingers were buried deep in her flaming hair. He lifted her bodily and from a long way off a door slammed shut and she felt the wind around them on the bridge between the towers.

The world fell away from beneath them, and the scent of the lemon trees rose in waves towards them.

"I shall ask Fabrizzi to paint you," Mark said deliberately. "I knew him in Rome before he became a lion of the art world. He told you, of course, that we met there?"

"Yes ... Mark, put me down! It makes me a little dizzy to look at everything without the handrail of the bridge to cling to."

"Cling to me," he said, and when his eyes met hers their quizzical deeps were as baffling as ever. "Put your arm about my neck – a little tighter than that, you ice-witch!"

He laughed and it rang out arrogantly on the bridge.

A strong, hard, relentless man like the land to which he belonged, which did not yield easily to the hand that would cultivate it.

Even now it made Ravena shy to touch him, and she wished as she felt the warm, hard nape of his neck that he would set her upon her feet. Someone below was looking up at them!

"Mark – it's Signor Fabrizzi!"

Stelio was waving to them, and she felt so self-conscious that she forced herself out of Mark's arms. "I – I must go and change into something less crumpled. I'll join you downstairs – " She hastened across the bridge to the door of the Knight's Tower and it was a relief to find herself in her own room, with the curtains wide open as she liked them, and a faint tang of polish mingling with the salty sea air.

She gave the bell-pull a tug and when the man-servant came she asked for hot water to be brought to her. It was a wonder Mark had not had hot water pipes laid in the tower. She would speak to him about it – and then was startled by the domestic trend of her thoughts, and the fact that she was thinking of herself as a wife who had the right to make such demands.

She put her hands to her cheeks and felt their warmth. Mark was home, and tonight he would make his own sort of demands. He would reawaken her to that wild, strange ecstasy that could not be called love, but was a hunger in him, a driving need to have from her a new child. A lusty son to place upon the great family bible downstairs, before the boy's name was entered therein.

Copper cans of steaming water were brought to her room, and she stripped behind the screen and washed from her slim body the dust and the musty memory of

Donata's honeysuckle scent. Draped in a towel, her red hair with its damp ends caping her, she stepped out from the shield of the screen and went to her wardrobe to select a dress. Stelio would stay for cocktails. He and Mark would discuss her portrait and when the sittings should start. She had not wanted to be painted, but all at once the idea was exciting. Perhaps in some primitive recess of her being she wanted to appear on canvas as a little lovelier than she was; a fairy-tale being who could also arouse worship.

She smiled as she caught sight of herself in the wardrobe mirror. She had the long slim legs of someone who liked to do a lot of walking, and feet with the small toes of a child. Her arms did not curve lusciously, and tendrils of her hair curled against her pale shoulders like tiny flames.

"What a pity," drawled a voice behind her, "that I could never allow you to be painted as you look right now."

A tremor passed down her body. Mark stood in the doorway of his room knotting the tie he had just put on. He had very much the look of a man who had the sole right to look at her *déshabille*.

"I have invited Fabrizzi to stay for dinner," he said.

"Oh – that's nice." Her hand clenched the skirt of a lemon-coloured dress with chiffon sleeves, for Mark had moved to her dressing-table to adjust his tie. He had every right to enjoy the privacy of her room, but she was still unbearably shy of him. She couldn't look at his wide shoulders without knowing that her head had lain against them, that her face had buried itself in the muscles that were clean and firm as steel.

"Would you like cocktails on the sea-terrace?" Mark turned to face her, and she flinched as always from the ravishment of the face that had been so fine.

"A-and something to eat." She forced a smile in case he had seen the way she flinched. "I can't wait until dinner time – I shall faint."

"You had no lunch?" His eyes narrowed sharply and he scanned her slim figure as if she might have lost weight and health since lunchtime.

"I told you," she gave a rueful laugh, "somebody locked me in the tower without even the traditional bread and water."

"Ravena," he came to her in one powerful stride and took hold of her, crushing her shoulders in the way of the strong who know their strength but don't use its full force, "I am sorry you missed your lunch and had this unnerving experience. It won't happen again! I shall speak to my grandmother in the severest terms."

"No, Mark." Ravena shook her head. "It will only make for more antagonism if you are stern with her."

"Antagonism?" he frowned. "You think it was that?"

"What else? Donna Jocasta wanted you to marry a girl of Sardinia, instead you bring home a stranger – someone she regards as an interloper. Perhaps she senses, Mark, that our marriage is not based on – love."

He gazed down at her, his brows a dark bar above his eyes, the man who had come to her and forced her into this marriage without a single tender word. She pulled away from him and turned to take her dress out of the wardrobe.

"How did you know I was in – the other tower?" she asked.

"The curtains were open." His eyes held a brooding look, and his voice echoed it. "You should not have gone there. The rooms are melancholy and should be shut up. I shall have to see about it." The next moment he had left the room in his abrupt way, leaving Ravena to change into her dress and to arrange her hair in a chignon at the nape of her neck. The neckline of her dress was a shallow scoop from her shoulders, emphasizing the youthful bloom of her skin and the fine bones beneath it. She studied herself in the mirror and decided to wear the pearl cross which Mark had given her. As she clasped the cross and chain about her throat, she wondered how she would ever grasp the complex essence of the man who was her husband.

She turned from the mirror, for what she saw there was the shape and not the essence of the woman who mattered to Mark. A young and spirited mother for the son he craved. A living son to wipe from his mind the memory of the child he had lost so cruelly.

Her fingers sought the pearl cross and found a measure of comfort and strength.

"We meet again, *madonna*." Stelio took her hand with his brilliant, flashing smile and touched his lips to the back of her wrist. "The *signor*, your husband, has been so good as to commission me to paint your portrait and I cannot wait to begin."

He flashed a smile at Mark, who drew forward a chair for Ravena, near the orange flowers that draped the sea-terrace wall. "The *signora* will not be an easy subject to put on canvas, but I enjoy a challenge."

"Why will she not be an easy subject?" Mark studied her in the lemon dress, set against the orange climbers, the reddening sun in her hair. "It appears to me that my wife has the colouring so much admired by Titian."

"Quite so," Stelio agreed. "And the eyes that change from sea-green to a mysterious woodland tint, according to her moods."

"I must promise to be in a good mood whenever I sit for you, *signore*." She felt shy of being discussed like this, as though she were an object, and was relieved when Renzio appeared with a tray of drinks and sandwiches. At his heels trotted the fawn, Bambo, and Ravena swooped on him with a croon of delight.

"He thinks he is a puppy dog, *signora*, and follows me about," Renzio said apologetically. "Shall I return him to the stables?"

Ravena smiled and caressed the fawn's soft ears. "Leave him with me, Renzio. He's so cute, isn't he?"

Renzio gave her a polite bow, but she caught the twinkle in his eye as he turned and left the terrace.

"You can hardly eat sandwiches with the fawn on your lap," Mark said quizzically. "And look, he's nuzzling your hair out of place."

"Now be still," she wagged a finger at the fawn, who settled down with his great mournful eyes fixed upon the orange flowers. "There," she said to Mark, "he'll be as good as gold."

Her husband's lips gave a quirk, and he placed sandwiches at her elbow on the terrace table.

"You will have a Martini, Signor Fabrizzi?"

"*Grazie*." Stelio accepted his drink and quizzed Ravena and her fawn. "I see now how I will paint you, with the dappled fawn on your lap, or perhaps at your feet."

"If he'll sit still long enough . . . mmm, these are delicious sandwiches. Won't you two men join me?"

Mark was lounging in a cane chair with his drink and he shook his head lazily. Stelio leaned against the terrace wall, a restless light in his eyes, as if he longed to start work on the new canvas. "Such an appetite, like an Italian girl," he chuckled, looking about him, taking note of the sea light that was thrown along the terrace even this late in the afternoon. "*Signore*, have I your permission to paint the portrait here on this terrace? I feel that the sky and the mountains will be the perfect background for Ravena."

The name slipped out, and Ravena was quick to notice the alert glint in Mark's eyes. "Very well," he said. "My wife is not a hot-house flower, but I draw the line at having her painted in a pair of trousers." His eyes met Ravena's, dark and demanding. "I like the dress you are wearing, *mia*. You will wear it for the portrait."

"Just as you say, Mark."

"With the red hair loosened and blowing a little in the wind," Stelio suggested. He took a deep breath of the tangy air and gazed with admiration at the view from the terrace. "*Bellissima*. Here is the real Sardinia. The heart of it, unspoiled by the bijou villas along the Emerald Coast. I pity myself that I live there rather than here."

"Surely you are free to live where you choose?" Ravena smiled at his extravagance, which matched his bold looks.

"An artist, *signora*," he had evidently caught the warning light in Mark's eye, "is at the mercy of commissions, and they come from the affluent, which gives me the means to paint the pastoral. Then again, I was an orphan in Naples, where I roamed the streets and lived on what I could pinch from the market stalls. A poor boy grows into a greedy man – that is, a man greedy for the things he lacked as a child."

"You mean, *signore*, that you can't resist luxury?"

He shrugged with Italian eloquence. "Let us say that

I cannot support the thought of poverty again. Until I was fifteen it was all I knew, then a famous artist came to Naples and he painted me on the waterfront, discovered that I had an eye for the artistic, and took me under his wing." Stelio glanced at Mark, and with some hesitation he added: "You knew that artist, Signor di Curzio. It was in his studio that we met for the first time."

"Yes. Will you have a cheroot?" Mark's face was without expression as he proffered his case, and then a light, to which Stelio lowered his handsome head with its crisply curling hair. Ravena watched the two men and she realized, with a tingling little shock, that there was not much difference in their actual ages, yet a world of difference lay between them. As a boy Mark had had all the things denied to Stelio ... as a man he had lost all that mattered to him.

They discussed the Sardinian countryside, and art, and touched on the Festa of Madri di Rosaria, which was due to take place in the hills.

"You will both attend, of course?" said Stelio.

"I have not visited the Chapel of Rosaria for several years." The smoke of Mark's cheroot veiled his eyes. "I think this year I will take Ravena."

"Rosaria, the Saint of Mothers." Stelio quizzed Ravena through his cheroot smoke. "And apart from that it is a real picnic *festa*, with fireworks and a barbecue, and a night spent on the mountainside."

Ravena listened absently to the two men, and watched the sun burn out of the sky. In a little while she suggested that they go indoors; it was growing chilly.

"Yes," Stelio tossed his cheroot stub to the rocks below and rubbed his hands together, "you certainly catch the wind from the mountains when the sun goes down. Being a warm-blooded Italian I feel the cold."

"There will be a fire in the *salottino*," Ravena assured him, and carrying her pet fawn she led the way indoors, and found herself hoping that Donna Jocasta would not join the dinner party. Her hope was realized. Baptista brought a note to Mark and then she scuttled away. He read it with a frown, tossed it into the fire and asked Ravena and their guest to excuse him for a few minutes.

There was silence for a second or two in the *salottino*, broken as a log sizzled and flared in the great fireplace.

"How do you get on with the old *padrona*?" Stelio asked.

Ravena looked pensive. "I'm afraid I don't. She is disappointed that Mark chose to marry a foreigner. She adored Donata, I think. She compares me with her."

"There is no comparison," Stelio said quietly.

"I know." Ravena knelt on the sheepskin rug in front of the fireplace and warmed her hands at the fire. "She was beautiful and she lacked none of the graces."

"But, Ravena," Stelio took hold of her and drew her to her feet. He studied her in the firelight, for the lamps had not yet been lit. "You have grace of spirit and you have it in full measure. You have also grace of body —"

"Stelio," she pulled away from him, alarmed in case Mark should reappear in his swift, noiseless way and find her close to the good-looking artist, "I want to be friends with you, but it won't be possible if you're going to say things — Mark wouldn't like."

"Must I pretend there was no yesterday?" he murmured. "When I saw you happier than you look today?

Are you only happy when your husband is not at home?"

"You have no right to say things like that!" Because he struck near the truth he made her angry. "You have been asked to paint my portrait, not to act as my analyst."

"An artist learns to read the eyes, and the eyes are the windows of the soul." His smile was unrepentant. "I wish our paths had crossed before Mark di Curzio entered your life. I think, *madonna*, that you and I would have found much to enjoy together."

"I think you presume on Mark's hospitality," she said stiffly. "I'm not one of your bored clients who fancies a flirtation with a good-looking artist, and I think it might be better if we called off the sittings."

"I think you would be sorry, afterwards," he said quietly.

"Sorry? What do you mean?"

"I think you need a friend, and I never supposed for one moment, Ravena, that you were like some of the other women who have sat for me. Yes, it pleased their ego to be painted by Fabrizzi, and it pleased their vanity to flirt with me. You are different. I like you and I want to paint you because you are a challenge. I wonder if I can transfer to canvas the sorcery that I see in you, and the element of sadness. It is no use to deny it." He shook his head at her. "How could it be otherwise for a young woman who must share her husband with a ghost?"

They stared at each other, she and Stelio, and suddenly the firelight was too intimate, it made the truth too easy to admit. She went from lamp to lamp and they bloomed ruby and gold and their cut-glass pendants swung from her touch.

"This is a beautiful room, isn't it?" She tried to sound like a young hostess proud of her home. "Do you see the way the carving on the cabinets catches the light, and the way the ceiling frescoes have kept their colour?"

They were discussing the frescoes when Mark returned, and Ravena saw from the drawn look of his brows that Donna Jocasta had annoyed him. He shook off the mood, however, and all through dinner he was charming ... reminding Ravena of how he had charmed Guardy when he dined at Ravenhall. With an anecdote that brought laughter, a slight turning of the head, he made one forget his fearful scars and was somehow fascinating.

Ravena toyed with the stem of her wine glass, and it seemed to her that it must have been a long time since someone had laughed as gaily as Stelio in this beautiful, sombre room. He was very attractive when he laughed and his white, rather boyish teeth gleamed against his Italian skin ... she would have to take care in the coming days not to show how much she liked the man with whom she would spend each afternoon on the sea-terrace.

"Bring Teo," she invited when they said good night. "He'll miss you otherwise."

"Your wife, *signore*," Stelio gave Mark a thoughtful smile, "has a compassionate heart. She is even thoughtful of my small dog, but I will bring him sometimes, with your permission?"

"Of course." Mark placed a firm arm about Ravena's waist and the light of the doorway lanterns was upon them as Stelio approached his sports car. Before sliding behind the wheel he turned to look at them.

"*Arrivederci!*" he called out, and then the night was alive with the roar of his engine and it was some minutes before quietness followed his departure.

The night was peaceful again, and there was the faintest of whispers in the dark green foliage of the cypress trees. A mass of lady's mantle cloaked a wall of the courtyard, and a pale glimmer came from the mysterious flowers that changed from blue to white when night fell.

"Flowers that, like our thoughts, change with the night," Mark murmured. "You are quiet, Ravena, and you make me curious about your thoughts."

"I – I hope everything was settled all right at the factory?" she said, and her eyes were upon their shadows merged by the lantern light.

"Yes, the matter of the new machinery is settled. Some of the workers are suspicious of modern methods – I told you, did I not, that the Sards like to cling to their old ways?"

"Mark," she tensed as she felt his hand smoothing her hair, "I hope you didn't have an argument with your grandmother? I'd hate to be the cause of a disagreement between you."

"Do you imagine," he laughed, "that *la nonna* and I have not had words before? We are both strong-willed, so of course we argue. We are fond of one another, so we soon forget and forgive. I told her that Signor Fabrizzi will be coming here each day to paint your portrait ... she called me a fool and said I should commission an artist who is less young and attractive."

With a swift movement he swung Ravena around so that she faced him and was encircled by his arms. "The honour of a Sard's house is in the keeping of his wife – do you understand me, Ravena?"

"I have never had trouble understanding you, Mark," she said, and then a sudden recklessness took hold of her. "What would you do if I betrayed you? That is – if you found out?"

The lantern light was in his eyes as they held hers. They glittered darkly and like pools with light on them, their depths could have been hiding anything.

"If a man made free with you," he said quietly, "I would ruin him. I would see to it that he lost everything he valued."

Light from the lanterns slanted across Mark's face, and his scars were etched with all the ruthlessness of his words. Ravena drew back from him with a cold little shiver, the green of her eyes flickering through her lashes. "Shall we go in?" she said.

"Yes." He followed her into the house and the great arched door closed with a clang. Then he took her by the hand and led her across the hall to the stairs. His hand holding hers was warm and strong, and as they mounted the stairs the shadows gradually enclosed them, and she remembered the night Mark had carried her up to the Knight's Tower, anger and passion in him.

Tonight his mood seemed gentler, but he went on holding her hand as if he expected her to run away from him.

CHAPTER SIX

THE time that followed fell into a pattern that was not unattractive.

Mark had promised Ravena a horse of her own to ride and he chose for her a glossy roan whose sire had been one of the stallions who ran wild in the hills of Sardinia. The colt was spirited but kind and Ravena soon made friends with him. Mark's favourite mount was a black Adonis with a streak of temper in him.

One morning she was down early at the stables for a romp with the foals, and she learned from one of the stable boys that Adonis had thrown his previous owner and trampled him.

"Adonis he don't like the whip," the boy explained. "But the *padrone* he never carry a whip, so the horse is good with him."

Ravena wondered how good as she stood at the half-door of Adonis' stall and held a sugar cube on her palm. His velvety nostrils gave a twitch, but he refused to accept the bribe from someone who was still a stranger to him.

"You arrogant devil," she laughed. "I wonder what you're like to ride?"

As the ward of a mounted Guardsman Ravena had been initiated into the joy and mystery of horseback riding when she was quite young. Both she and Rhodri had been taught properly, and Ravena had what was called "a good seat". She never slumped in the saddle and rode with an easy grace which had pleased Mark. The fact that he had given her a colt with spirit was proof that he liked her riding. She was aware that her Sardinian husband rarely paid compliments in the small coin of words and was in every way a man of action.

As she stood admiring Adonis, she heard booted feet crossing the stableyard and she swung round, clad lightly in riding trousers and a check shirt. Mark always looked younger and very athletic in his riding outfit. In fact she had never known a man as fit and hard as her husband. He took long hours of work in his stride, was often late at his desk going through piles of paperwork, and was also active in local affairs.

"Good morning." She smiled with that persistent shyness of him clutching at her heart. "I've been trying to make friends with Adonis, but he seems shy of me."

Mark quirked a black brow. "I hope you don't try to venture into his stall? He was once badly treated and remains suspicious of most people."

"I hate to think of anyone hurting such a proud creature," she said.

Her husband's smile was quizzical as he swung open the door of Adonis' stall and entered with a few throaty Sardinian words. Ravena handed him the sugar, which the horse took with a rough, loving thrust of his head against Mark's shoulder. As he was saddled and bridled, Mark spoke to him in that low, throaty voice, and Ravena thought how well they were matched. They shared the dark memory of pain, and were supple and dangerous and hard to get close to.

Then she heard hoofbeats on the cobbles and the friendly nicker of her colt as he was led from his stall, saddled for their morning ride. She ran to mount him and the morning sun was agleam on her hair and the glossy coat of her horse. He pricked his ears and shook his bridle, as if to say, "Come on, let's be off!"

She turned to see if Mark was in the saddle, and he was, his wide-brimmed hat pulled forward to shadow his dark face. They cantered from the stableyard and the wind met them as they came out upon the open countryside.

To ride across the wild land was to feel free, though Mark rode beside her. There was a spell upon the mornings, as tangible as the scent of herbage and the dew that clung sparkling to the tall blades of grass and the thistle-stalks. Later the sun would drain the colour out of the grass and the wild flowers, but as yet the sun was a caress and not a conqueror's touch.

Her heart sang a strange song, half joy, half wonderment that she felt so near to happiness. The wind whipped her hair into a red pennant, and she strove to race Mark across the land whose every rock and shadow and bent olive-tree was known to him. Was she trying to escape him? She turned to look at him and saw his teeth flash white against his sunburnt skin. He was holding Adonis back, letting her believe that she could get away from him. His hat on its neck cord had blown to the back of his head and he might have been a brigand in pursuit of her.

A thrill of fear sang through her veins; a thrill as old as time, and she urged her colt to a swifter pace, her knees gripping the saddle as he took a track that led downwards, towards the dense green of a pine forest. She heard the stones of the track scattering beneath Adonis' hooves, and then her colt reached the mossy path that led through the forest and the scent of the resin took her breath and seemed to intoxicate her and the colt.

It was when they came to a stream, a gush of silvery

water in the heart of the forest, that the colt suddenly balked, coming to a standstill so suddenly that Ravena was almost tossed out of the saddle. She sat winded and breathless, cloaked in pine shadows as Mark galloped up beside her.

"That was – *good*," she said breathlessly. "Is that water all right to drink, Mark?"

"It comes down from the mountains, sweet and wild," he said.

She cast him a quick look, then slid from the saddle. She ran to kneel among a bank of ferns and cupped her hands for a drink of stream water, It was as cooled as if iced and she gasped as it ran chilly and delicious down her throat.

"Aren't you thirsty?" she inquired of Mark, who had dismounted and stood leaning against a pine tree, the shadowy greenness half-masking his lean face.

"I could drink some coffee," he said, and she felt him looking at her as she sat by the stream and dried her hands on the ferns. "Would you like to go and have breakfast at a little *trattoria* I know of? They will have sardines straight out of the sea, grilled and stuffed with herbs."

"Mmmm, I am hungry," she admitted. "Riding always whips up my appetite."

"You love to ride, don't you, Ravena?"

"I never rode such a fine horse before." She eyed her colt with affection, and looked about her at the tall, resinous pine trees and slithers of sunshine in which butterflies danced. A warm, green dusk filtered through the forest and the shifting light on the leaves and on the surface of the stream was like the enigmatic lights and shadows of Mark's eyes.

"I love the scent of pine," she said. "It's so fresh and

tangy, like a swift ride through the wind, like cool water, and everything with a bite to it."

She looked at Mark and saw the glimmer of his teeth in a faint smile, and she realized how alone they were. He was her husband, yet still he was the one person who could set her nerves tingling. A ray of sunshine touched the raven darkness of his hair. His shoulders were wide and supple beneath the white shirt. His limbs were long and his knee-boots added to his look of male strength. To reach her horse she had to pass him, and her heart drummed as she rose to her feet and made herself walk towards him.

He reached out a lazy hand and drew her against him. His other hand lost itself in her windblown hair and his lips touched hers, cool from the water of the stream.

Suddenly his grip tightened and he spoke against her mouth. "You kiss as if you had ice in your veins, and you look as if you had fire. Not once, Ravena, in our weeks together, have you kissed me with warmth."

"I've given all I have to give," she said, and the chill on her lips was in her voice. "If you wanted love – if you wanted that, Mark, then you should not have forced me into marrying you."

"Would you have listened if I had courted you in the conventional manner?" he asked, a note of irony in his voice. "What did you think when we first met?"

"I hoped you would go away and never return," she said, and her heart beat so close to his that she knew he felt its wild racing.

"It was as if the devil had come to you in person eh?" He touched her face, tracing the delicate bone beneath the smooth skin. "Have I been such a devil to you, Ravena? Have I made you so unhappy? A while ago your eyes were sparkling."

"I– I like to ride. It was good of you to give me a horse I can ride well."

"You must have learned as a child?"

"Yes. Guardy always treated me as if I were his daughter and the things Rhodri had were never denied to me. We went to riding school together –"

"You were together a lot?"

She glanced up at Mark and saw that his eyes had hardened. "As I said once before, Mark, I can't wipe out the memory of Rhodri as I knew him. So gay and debonair in his uniform. Charming –"

"Charming?" Mark laughed on a low bitter note, and let her go. "Come, let us go and have breakfast!"

They remounted and made their way out of the pine forest. The sun struck warmer as they wended their way down a path to the tiny inn tucked away on the cliffs above the sea. It had roughcast walls of white, a sloping roof of coloured shingles, and a garden deep in vines and fig-trees, and a huge mulberry-tree with tables beneath its boughs.

They were shown to one of these tables by a lean young man with a shy smile, who spoke broken English and was so eager in all his movements that he knocked over the salt-pot as he flicked open a napkin and spread it on Ravena's lap. "*Si, si, signore,*" blushing and smiling he threw pinches of salt over his left shoulder. "Here come the sardines now, fresh from the sea."

A young woman with bare brown feet and a scarlet skirt appeared in the garden, a fish basket slung over her shoulder. "*Buon giorno, padrone!*" she flashed a smile at Mark, and eyed Ravena with curiosity. "You come to eat our grilled sardines, like in the old days?"

"*Si*, Santuzza. I bring my wife to eat the tastiest

breakfast in all Sardinia."

"You are kind to say so, *signore*." The young woman dropped him a curtsey, and Ravena was struck by her bold, laughing eyes in a sun-browned face. Her blue blouse and scarlet skirt made her as vivid as a painting, and Ravena noticed that she looked at Mark as if they were old friends.

She carried her fish basket into the inn, and Mark ordered two glasses of buttermilk while they waited for their sardines to be cooked. An old woman brought the brimming glasses, and like so many of the older generation she wore a black scarf over her head.

"I remember, *padrone*, when you bring the little wild hawk to drink our buttermilk. *Questa la vita*, eh?" She scanned Ravena with deep-set eyes, taking in her red hair and her white skin with the deliberateness of the elderly. "A pretty piece, yes; a man's head could be turned, but it is better for us to keep to our own."

Muttering, clicking her beads, she ambled away and Ravena was left staring at Mark. "*Questa la vita?*" she murmured.

"Such is life, *mia*." He stared back at her as if the old woman's words had made him remember too vividly the other times when he had come to the inn, bringing a dark-haired girl to eat breakfast with him beneath the silk tree; and bringing later his small son – the little wild hawk – whose looks might have reminded the man of the mother.

Ravena sipped her buttermilk and sought wildly for something to say. Oh, why had Mark brought her here? Why, when this inn garden was shadowed by memories for him; when he must hear again the laughter of a child hiding among the vines and the fig-trees that were bent like witches?

"Mark –"

"It's all right, Ravena." His smile was a twist of the lip. "I thank you for the look in your eyes – the pity for a child. He loved to come here, to hide among the trees and to splash the water of that old fountain. But as you say, memories cannot be wiped away, nor can one go on hiding from them – ah, here comes Natalina with our sardines!"

The plump sardines had been grilled over charcoal and were crisp on the plate and bursting with a herb stuffing. Crusty bread and creamy butter were served with them, and Natalina's scarlet skirt whirled like a dancer's as she moved from one side of the table to the other. Her brother brought the coffee and received a scolding for spilling coffee in Ravena's saucer.

"He talks of being a waiter in the city," she scoffed. "Carlu, there would be a hundred strangers for you to stare at in the city! To think of what would happen when you served spaghetti!"

"Be quiet, Natalina," he begged. He was scarlet and he almost dropped the cream jug when Ravena gave him a quick, sympathetic smile from eyes as green as gems. The cream made a zigzag pattern on the surface of her coffee.

"*Grazie*," she murmured.

"You are welcome, *signorina*." He gave her a jerky bow. "You have all you require? You have only to say –?"

"I have all I want, thank you, Carlu."

Her use of his name seemed to stun him, and when his sister pinched his arm he turned on her with a furious remark in Sardinian. Mark's eyebrow was quirked in amusement as the brother and sister disappeared into the inn in a volley of words.

"You have awoken hidden fires," he chuckled."Nata-lina will find that young man less easy to boss now he has been smiled at by you."

"Is my smile so inflammable?" It was a relief that Mark was looking less tense – and the sardines were deliciously crisp and tasty.

"You must know by now," he said mockingly, "that you have only to smile to make a man your slave."

"You – a slave?" She glanced up and laughed out-right, her green eyes flicking his shoulders, taking in his look of aloofness. "You told me that Sards bowed down to no one, and I certainly believe it of you. Mmmm, I've never tasted sardines as good as these before! And the bread – it's still warm from the oven and the butter melts on it!"

"You look like a hungry schoolgirl," he said.

And indeed, with her wind-tangled hair, her check shirt open at the throat, and a chunk of bread and butter in her hand, Ravena hardly looked a wife. Only the gold ring on her left hand gave away the fact and she knew that Mark was comparing her to Donata. She would always have looked cool and lovely and poised. Her dark hair would always have been smooth, her eyes ready with a smile for him, her voice soft with seduction.

Ravena wiped her lips, and perhaps she stifled the cry that came from her heart. Mark had known love ... but he had robbed her of the joy of ever knowing it. She had only his passion!

"What will you eat now, girl-bride?" He rose lazily from his chair and approached a sunlit wall on which rusty-gold pomengranates were half-hidden among their leaves. "Shall we share Persephone's fruit?"

She watched him cut the fruit in half and saw the

juice run across his scarred hand. "Do you know the legend of Persephone?" he asked

Ravena took a bite of the sweet fruit. "Aidoneus came upon her while she was picking flowers and he carried her off to his palace ... will I, at the end of six months, be allowed to return to my own world for a while?"

"If you wished to see your guardian I would not stop you." Mark looked at her with dark eyes. "Or is it the charming Rhodri whom you long to see?"

"Please – do we have to talk about him?" She jumped to her feet and walked away among the fig-trees and the crowding vines. The grapes were small, bitter as yet, and there was an arbour holding a small iron seat. She sat down and twisted her handkerchief in her fingers. She didn't look up when Mark's tall figure darkened the entrance.

"We must go home," he said.

Home? What poignant visions she had when she thought of going home ... to her room over the deep porch of Ravenhall, with its circular window and its deep recess. Her books, her oddments, her privacy enclosed by white-painted walls.

"Come," said Mark, and she felt trapped ... there was no way out of the arbour except into his arms.

"I hate you!" The words broke from her. "I shall never feel anything else, for you or that fortress on a hill and the everlasting wind in the cypress trees. They sound at night as if they were weeping ... did anything, or anyone, ever do anything else at the Casa Cipresso? Was it ever a happy house?"

"You are being very young." He drew her to her feet, and when she tried to pull away from him, he exerted his easy strength and she found herself back in his arms.

"This is what you like, isn't it?" she said bitterly. "You like proving that I can't get away from you."

He laughed without humour and tipped her face towards him. "How green and stormy your eyes are," he murmured.

"Don't!" She twisted her head away from him, for she was sure he meant to kiss her.

He merely laughed again and his scarred hand ran in a single caress down the length of her red hair.

"Come, let us go back," he said, and this time he did not refer to the house of the cypress as home.

Stelio arrived after lunch to continue with her portrait, but after about an hour he threw down his brush and strode to the table on which stood a jug of the iced pineapple he liked to drink while working.

"Today I have a changeling on my hands," he frowned. "Will you have a glass of juice?"

She shook her head and relaxed against the parapet of the sea-terrace. They had found that the fawn would not keep still, that he was distracting, so Stelio painted her standing alone by the parapet. So far the portrait had gone well. Today ... he shrugged his shoulders and gave her a long, searching look.

"What has upset you?" he demanded. "You have become again a stranger to smiling, and I insist on having that Mona Lisa smile of yours in my portrait of you."

"One can't always smile," she rejoined. "I – I have a slight headache."

"Are you being honest with me?" He walked towards her, a lithe, brown-skinned figure in needlecord slacks and a pale blue shirt. The breeze ruffled his hair, and there were little amber lights in his brown eyes. "Is it perhaps your heart that aches?"

She was startled by his perception and keenly aware that she had to be careful with Stelio. He was very attractive, and he was also sympathetic, and right now Ravena longed for a little sympathy. For a shoulder to prop herself against, if only for a few restful moments. She turned away from the temptation and gazed at the mountains, and at the silvery scrolls of water far below the house. They pulsed like the waves of a heartbeat, one after the other, eternal. And there was heat in the air, as if a storm might be brewing.

"The atmosphere is heavy," she said. "It makes me restless."

Stelio came and stood beside her. "It's the sirocco perhaps, a hot wind that blows in from Africa and which always has a nervous effect on a stranger. All the same –"

"Don't say it, Stelio," she said tensely.

"I have been wanting to say it for the past hour. You are unhappy, Ravena, and I know the cause."

"You couldn't possibly know it." She forced a smile and looked at him. "It's too warm and sticky for any more work. Stelio, take me for a drive!"

"I would like to." Amber lights burned in his eyes. "What of your husband?"

"Mark is at a meeting of wine-makers. He won't be back for hours and I – I want to feel the wind on my face."

"Then come!" Stelio caught at her hand and like a couple of children let out of school they raced down the stairs and across the hall and out of the door. Neither of them noticed the dark-clad figure lurking about on the gallery, a shadow with gleaming eyes, who hastened to tell her mistress that the *padroncina* had just gone running from the house, gay as a lark, with the handsome Italian painter.

His car was a cream-coloured Lotus and in no time at all they were driving through the wind on the mountain roads. Each time they took a curve, Ravena caught her breath and felt a sense of elation. She would worry about taking this drive when it was over; right now she wanted only to enjoy herself.

"It feels good, eh?" Stelio yelled above the rush of wind.

"Wonderful," she laughed. "You should be a racing driver."

He shot her a swift smile. "The wind whips your hair like a pennant of silk. Ravena, I have an idea – shall we drive down to the coast?"

"N-no, it's too far."

"Not in Lottie! I can give you an iced beer at my place and have you home again by six o'clock."

Again she caught the flash of his teeth. "Scared?"

"Of you?" she scoffed.

"No – of your husband."

Fingers seemed to clutch her heart, and the very fact that she was afraid of Mark made her rebellious. "All right, you can treat me to an iced beer," she said recklessly. "No, on second thoughts – "

"Too late," he laughed. "We are now on the coast road."

"I was merely going to say that I prefer orangeade."

The sports car sped along a smooth ribbon of road that edged the sea for some miles, but it was some time before apprehension relaxed its grip on Ravena. She knew she was doing the wrong thing – as far as Mark was concerned – and she decided to keep from him this visit to Stelio's villa. What he didn't know he wouldn't worry about!

Along this coastal road grew prickly pear-trees and bamboos, rustling in the hot wind and golden against the blue of the sea. They began to pass white-stoned villas nestling among flowers and almond-trees, and soon they mounted a slight gradient and Stelio swung the car into the paved *piazzetta* of one of the most attractive houses she had ever seen.

A white, arabesqued stairway led to a terrace; there were green jalousies at the windows and a red-tiled roof caught the sun. It was a gay little house, exactly the sort of place for an artist who was also a bachelor.

"Well?" He sat with an elbow on the wheel and quizzed her face. "Are you coming in?"

"How can I resist?" She slid out of the car and he came round to her from the other side. They walked up the stairway to the terrace and he unlocked the door with a small yale key. The room they entered was spacious and cool, with honey-coloured furniture, a half-moon couch of orange velvet, a few copper ornaments, and a drinks cabinet in Persian walnut with ebony-framed doors. Here and there on the plain walls were Italian prints, and a little antique casket stood on a low table with a cigarette-lighter in the form of a swan.

"How – sybaritic," Ravena said with a smile.

"I was a deprived youth, remember." He looked boldly into her eyes. "Please sit down and I'll pour you a drink."

"Make it an orangeade," she said lightly, and sat down in one of his deep velvet chairs, the lemon of her dress mingling pleasantly with the orange velvet. She put up a hand to tidy her hair and saw Stelio run his glance over her, before he turned to the Persian cabinet. He opened one of the doors and looked inside. "I am all out of orangeade," he said. "Won't you trust me and have a gin and tonic?"

"Make it a tonic with ice." She looked at the gold ring on her left hand and her gaze was curiously thoughtful. "Do you live all alone, Stelio?" she asked.

"Yes, don't you feel sorry for me? A woman comes in to clean and polish for me, and when I have guests she cooks for me, but most evenings I go to a restaurant for my dinner."

"Always alone?" Ravena taunted as she accepted her tonic and ice in a tulip-shaped glass.

He sat down on the half-moon sofa with his own drink, and hitched his slacks so he could cross his legs. "*Saluta*," he raised his glass and took a deep swallow. "A man gets lonely and there is only one remedy for that – anyway, do I look the sort who could live like a monk?"

She smiled and shook her head. "I always thought that Italians married young and had large families."

"There are exceptions to every rule. Take yourself," he said deliberately, "a pretty girl married against her will."

The smile froze on her lips. "I didn't come here to talk about my marriage. I came –"

"To forget it for a while," he broke in. "Ravena, you don't have to pretend with me. I have seen how you are with me when I paint you, and how you look when Mark di Curzio joins us on the terrace of the Casa. It is as if a little light goes out in your eyes ... as if you dare not be yourself –"

"Stop it!" She set aside her half-finished drink and jumped to her feet "I didn't come here to have my marriage analysed, or my personal feelings discussed. They're no business of yours!"

"You think not?" He rose also and never had she

127

seen him look so serious. "We met on a beach and I thought you charming. We met again at di Curzio's house and I saw an entirely different girl from the one who explored the blue grotto with me. Each day since we have met and I have tried to transmit the laughing lights I saw in your eyes into my painting of you – it is impossible! They are no longer there. Something has quenched them."

He tossed back the remainder of his drink. "*Madonna*, do you take me for a fool? Do you think I have seen so little of the world that I don't know an unhappy woman when I see one?"

"Did you think I came here today to be consoled?" she demanded. "Is that how unhappy clients usually react to *your* charms?"

"You admit you are unhappy?" His eyes held hers as he bent to take a cigarette from the antique casket. She shook her head as he proffered the box, and went to the long glass doors through which a puff of hot air came and made her feel breathless. The trees and flowers stirred sluggishly and the sun looked bruised.

She tensed as Stelio came and stood at her shoulder, but her awareness of him was not physical, it was that she felt him to be kind and kindness was a dangerous quality when a woman was in need of it.

"How quiet everything is," she said. "Even the cicadas are becalmed and the trees seem embroidered against the hot blue of the sky."

"I like the way you say things," he murmured. "You have a fey quality I have never met in any other woman."

"Have you known many, Stelio?"

"I am thirty-two, and to be a painter of worth a man must know people."

"I'm sorry you are having trouble with my portrait – perhaps you should abandon it."

"To abandon the painting would be to abandon you." His breath stirred against her hair. "Ravena, you have enchanted me – please, don't move away! I am not going to touch you, or force you to share my feelings. I know you are a girl to be faithful to your husband even though you don't love him – one day, perhaps, you will tell me why you married him."

She shivered ... perhaps it was the growl of thunder, the flicker of steel in the sky that made her draw back sharply from the windows. This brought her close to Stelio and they touched without volition, and the next instant he caught hold of her and pressed a kiss to her temple. She closed her eyes and the memory of Guardy rushed over her. So kind and guarding, kissing her on the temple when she ran in from school ...

Tears filled her eyes and rolled down her face, while outside the clouds suddenly burst and a torrent of rain roared down out of the sky. It splashed through the open glass doors and Stelio drew her away from them. The room darkened and the air seemed to hum with tension.

"I – I shouldn't have come here." Ravena brushed at her wet cheek and gazed wildly at the storm. "How long will it last – Stelio, I have to get home!"

"I cannot take you in this." He looked appalled. "You have no idea how bad those mountain roads can be in a downpour. Relax, *carina*. Such heavy rain cannot last long and I will take you home as soon as possible."

She began to pace to and fro, flinching as lightning cut the stormy dusk light in the lounge. Why had she agreed to come here? She had known she was doing wrong ... now they were trapped by the storm and it seemed as if the fury of the rain would never cease.

"Sit down." He made her do so and poured her a fresh drink. She knew the moment her lips touched it there was gin in it, but she drank it and felt her head swim slightly. She was hot and her heart pounded. She was afraid ... for herself and for Stelio.

"Mark will be so angry," she said. "I never meant to tell him I came here with you."

"What can he do?" Stelio was leaning towards her from the other chair. "What sort of man would be angry to be told the truth – that we have had a drink, that we have talked, that we are friends?"

"It's hard to explain – "

"Try, Ravena. Make me understand why a girl such as yourself must go in fear of a man who should feel only love for you, only a desire to make you happy."

"Mark doesn't bully me." She tried to smile, but it was a poor effort. "Sometimes he can be – fascinating."

"Did you mistake fascination for love?" Stelio persisted.

"Love?" She stared at the rain, which fell so hard that it sounded like so many whiplashes across the paving of the terrace. Stelio had closed the glass doors almost together and the air was stifling.

"When life hurts you badly, you stop believing in love," she said quietly. "Mark never asked for my love, and I married him because there was nothing else to do but let him have his way."

"Why, because you felt compassion for him?" Stelio caught at her left hand and fingered her gold ring. "Because you could not bear to hurt a man who had been hurt already? Ravena, a marriage such as yours is a sacrifice!"

Her face in the storm light was pensive; her eyes were like dark green pools. Yes, a sacrifice! It couldn't be denied, but neither could she allow Stelio to play on her need for sympathy. She had to fight such a weakness in herself, or she would end up in his arms!

"When I was a child," she said, forcing a light note into her voice, "and the rain stopped me from going out, I used to say a rhyme: 'Rain, rain, go away. Come again some other day'. There, do you think the spell will work?"

"I think there is every chance." Stelio's fingers gripped hers. "I have never met anyone who could cast such a spell as you ..."

At that precise moment the door chimes echoed through the villa. Thunder growled and lightning flicked its knife-edge across Stelio's eyes as he and Ravena stared at one another. His eyes were alert with the alarm that flickered through Ravena.

CHAPTER SEVEN

"Who could be calling in a storm?" Stelio frowned. He let go of her hands and rose to his feet as the chimes rang out once again. "I must answer the door, Ravena."

"Of course," she said, and again their eyes met and held a single question. He shrugged slightly and strode from the room, and she listened tensely to catch the visitor's voice when Stelio opened the front door. She felt as guilty as if she and Stelio were clandestine lovers . . . as if Mark himself had come for her.

She was staring at the door of the lounge when a tall, rainwet figure appeared in the aperture and her deepest fear was realized.

"Ravena!" he exclaimed and the rain dripped into his eyes from his black hair as he raked her slender figure in the deep velvet chair. She couldn't move; her position was as if too comfortable for movement. Her green eyes were fixed on Mark's stony face.

It was incredible and yet it was real . . . Mark had come for her!

He walked into the room and Stelio followed him. He looked boyish beside Mark and a nerve twitched in his temple when the tall, grim-faced man swung round to face him.

"I should like an explanation," he said in a voice that was cold and yet with the heat of anger beneath. "What is my wife doing here?"

The rain pounded the terrace and a small enamelled clock chimed out the hour, as if underlining the fact that Ravena should have been in her own home at this time of day and not cosily ensconced with an artist whose reputation was rather rakish.

"What are you doing here?" she asked Mark. "Did someone at the Casa see me leave with Stelio? Did you come here to drag me away?"

He shot her a black look. "No," he said. "My car broke down not far from here and I knew that Signor Fabrizzi was on the telephone. I was going to ask permission to phone a garage ... I had no idea that I would find my wife with the *signor*."

There was one of those silences in which innocence took on the look of guilt and only the sound of rain could be heard. Ravena could not resist a glance of appeal at Stelio, and when he cleared his throat to speak it seemed to add to the guilty atmosphere.

"The air was so sultry that we took a drive," Stelio said. "It was I who persuaded Ravena to come here for a drink – and then the storm came and I had to convince her that it would be madness to drive up into the mountains in such a downpour. If it had not been for the storm –"

"You would have driven her home and I should not have known that she had been here," Mark cut in. He look at Ravena and his eyes were without illusion. He knew she wouldn't have told him, and as he took a step towards her, she retreated as if she feared he might touch her.

"Do we have to make such a drama out of this?" she said defiantly. "I have had one drink and that a tonic with ice."

Mark glanced at the tulip glass on the table beside the chair in which she had been sitting. He picked it up and inhaled from it, and she remembered that the glass had held a finger of gin. Mark replaced the glass so that it rang on the surface of the table. "Is the portrait of my wife almost completed?" he demanded of Stelio.

"The portrait is a failure," Stelio rejoined. "I thought in the beginning that Ravena would be a happy subject to paint, but now I know that she is an unhappy woman and I cannot get on to canvas the reality of her. I can no more do that than you can possess the heart of her, Signor di Curzio."

The two men faced each other, while lightning flickered into the room like the steel of crossed foils.

"Do you imagine *you* have her heart?" Mark looked and spoke sardonically. "You flatter yourself, *signore*. The man who has Ravena's heart is far from here. She can forgive him his sins, and a woman can do that for a man she loves."

Stelio looked at her and his eyes were bewildered. "Ravena –"

"I want to go home," she said, and she was looking at Mark. "I've not afraid of the mountain roads, so telephone the garage and have them fix your car."

"Take mine!" There was a hardness in Stelio's voice. "Here are the keys." He took them from his pocket and tossed them to Mark. "I have to come to the Casa tomorrow to collect my painting gear and I will get someone to bring me by boat. I can drive home again in the Lotus."

He was challenging Mark, daring him to drive the Lotus in the storm, on roads where landslides occurred when it rained heavily. He looked at Ravena and his eyes were disenchanted.

She said nothing, certain that Mark would accept the challenge.

"Will you lend my wife a coat?" he said to Stelio.

The painter inclined his head and went out of the room to fetch one. Mark jingled the car keys in his hand.

"Are you nervous?" he asked Ravena.

"Would it matter to you if I were, Mark?"

He stared at her and lightning flickered between them. "I have always admired your courage," he said. "The one thing I can't stop being amazed at is that a girl of courage should love a coward –"

There he broke off as Stelio returned with a raincoat. Mark took it and swung it about Ravena's shoulders like a cloak.

"*Signore*," Stelio's hard look had turned to a troubled one, "please won't you both stay here until the storm abates? There is food enough in the ice-box –"

"Stelio," Ravena gripped the edges of his raincoat, "once Mark has made up his mind to do something, no one can turn him from his purpose. If I pleaded –" she looked at Mark. "No, I shall never again plead for anything from Mark."

She walked to the door and she looked very slender and lost in the long raincoat. "Shall we go, Mark? Soon it will be quite dark."

The rain fell insistently and the wheels of the car hissed as they swept down the gradient on which the villa stood. Ravena stared through the windscreen, across which the wipers swept like the spokes of a fan. Mark drove with assurance, not speaking, his dark eyes fixed upon the road ahead.

It shook her when about half an hour later he brought the car to a screeching halt on a grass verge just below the mountains. He turned to her and the small overhead light shone in a sinister way on his scarred face. "I can't do it!" He spoke savagely, and looked at his hands, which slowly clenched so that the burn scars stood out lividly. "It would be madness on a night like this –"

Ravena's eyes were fixed upon his face and she knew what fearful memory was gripping him, making it impossible for him to drive on. He was remembering Dresti, trapped in the wreckage of that other car.

Suddenly he reached out and drew the raincoat about her. She looked small and lost in its folds. "We must stay here a while," he said, and then a sudden gleam came into his eyes. "No, I remember there is a shepherd's hut not far from here! Come, we may get a supper of stewed lamb if we are lucky!"

They ran across the field through the rain, his arm slung about her, the raincoat flapping about her ankles. There it stood, the conical *pinnedda* with its single room, its air of isolation amidst the storm. Mark tried the door and it opened easily ... but there was no cheery fire, no stewpot simmering above the flames. The lightning flickered in and revealed a bench with a bundled sheepskin on it, a three-legged stool, and a crooked stave leaning against one of the stone walls. The wind blew a gust of rain against the hut. The stave fell with a clatter and Ravena gave a nervous jump.

"Go in." Mark struck a match and played the small light round the abandoned hut. There on the hearth was some kindling, and stuck in the neck of a wine-bottle was part of a candle. Mark lit the wick, which spluttered and burned rather dismally, causing shadows to dance up the walls.

The rain pounded the roof, and Ravena looked at Mark as he stood shielding the candle flame with his hand.

"Close the door," he said.

"You mean," she gave a slight shiver, "we're going to stay here?"

"There is nothing else we can do at present." He reached out and closed the door himself. "Strange shelter for two on a stormy night, but it will suffice. We can light a fire –" His eyes met and held hers. "Are you afraid to be alone with me when you would have dared that drive in the storm?"

"I – I'm afraid there might be mice –"

"Fieldmice won't hurt you." His smile was sardonic as he found a wall niche in which to place the candle. It burned fitfully and Mark's shadow towered up the wall as he went to the hearth to see how much kindling there was.

"The wood is dry and should burn quite well – come, Ravena, we will make ourselves cosy enough before the night is over."

She plunged shaky hands into the pockets of Stelio's raincoat, for never before had she been so entirely alone with Mark. He was her husband, yet still he was the one man who could make her feel shy and intensely aware of herself as a woman.

A weakness seemed to take hold of her and she leaned against the door, which rattled in the gusts of wind.

"Don't stand there in the draught." Mark's eyes seemed to hold twin flames as he turned to look at her. "Come here to me, Ravena."

She obeyed as if she had no will of her own left. She felt his hands touch her hair. "Your hair is damp from the rain," he said. "I will light that fire at once."

His own hair lay in damp, black clusters above his eyes ... such night-dark hair and eyes ... such arms of steel crushing her against the lean length of him. She

137

felt she would faint as his lips brushed the hollow of her throat ... her heart seemed to turn over as he buried his face against her throat.

It was then, in that strange shelter on the moor, that Ravena had her first intimation that Mark was to get what he desired so much from her, and as her legs gave way, he lifted her and carried her to the bench and laid her down on the sheepskin.

"It's all right," he stroked the hair off her forehead. "I am not angry any more about finding you with Fabrizzi. Poor child, you are worn out!"

"Mark –"

"Ssh. Rest while I light the fire."

He went over to the hearth and began to lay the pieces of kindling one across the other, then he sought about in his pockets for a piece of paper to place beneath the wood to help it catch alight. Ravena watched as he drew a letter out of his pocket and scanned it. She heard him catch his breath, then he screwed the sheet of paper into a ball, placed it beneath the wood and applied a match to it.

As it burned and the dry kindling gave a crackle, he stared at the flames and seemed struck into the immobility of a statue.

Suddenly Ravena sat up ... suddenly she wanted to know what had been in the letter he had just burned. "Mark, what's wrong?" she demanded. "Please look at me – tell me!"

He straightened up and as he turned in the candlelight his face was a dark mask. "I will tell you tomorrow," he said, and the warmth had gone out of his voice.

"No, tell me now." She slid off the bench and came to him. She glanced at the fire in which the letter had burned to ashes, then she searched his face and felt the hammering of her heart.

"It was a letter to Rhodri Brenin which I found in your room some time ago," he said harshly. "A letter you never sent, in which you wrote of your meeting with him on *our* wedding day. Shall I quote your words, Ravena?"

Her hand was at her throat, which he had kissed such a short while ago. She could feel the pounding beneath the soft skin.

"The letter is burned, but not the words." Mark's voice softened in a dangerous way. " '*I had to see you once more and I am not sorry, even though Mark was very angry. Those hours with you have helped me to face what would otherwise have been an impossible situation. Our bond of love ensures secrecy. I can cling to that whenever I feel afraid of the deep water into which I have leapt . . .*'

"There the letter broke off," Mark said grimly. "You never finished it. Was it so unbearable to send him a letter when you longed to be with him? Writing of those hours you spent with him on *our* wedding day must have tormented you, so you screwed up the letter, threw it from you, and never gave it a thought that your husband might pick it up out of curiosity."

She stared at Mark and knew that he had misunderstood ever word in that reckless letter which she should have burned herself. *Those hours with you.* Words that conveyed only one meaning to Mark . . . he thought that she and Rhodri had been lovers!

There had to be some way to deny this, but she saw from the hard, bitter line of his mouth that he would be scornful of whatever she said. She shivered as the wind howled around the *pinnedda* and threw gusts of woodsmoke into the room. Mark picked up the wooden stave and thrust it up the chimney, dislodging the soot that clogged it. The soot showered down and sparked as it burned, and the smell mingled with that of rain and fleece and the earth-floor.

"I am sorry we have nothing to eat or drink, but better for you to be a little hungry than to be involved in a car accident on a mountain road." Mark sought about in his pockets and brought out his cheroot-case. "One of these would make you dizzy – do you mind if I smoke?"

"Please smoke," she said, and heard the little note of desperation in her voice. Perhaps then he would relax and not stand towering over her.

He fired a cheroot, blew out the match and puffed a plume of smoke without taking his eyes from hers. She couldn't bear the intensity of the gaze that sought to read her mind, and she went to the little three-legged stool and drew it near to the fire. She sat down and warmed her hands.

"I'm not in the least hungry," she said. "Though a cup of tea would be nice."

The smoke of Mark's cheroot curled into the air like a blue question-mark. The firelight played on the rough walls of their refuge. "*La nonna* will be worried about us," he said. "Why did you not stay at home? I could have driven home alone – it would not have mattered."

"You would risk your own life?" Ravena said tensely.

He shrugged. "I could not risk yours – my dear, don't look alarmed! I am not about to declare my deathless love for you. You are young ... Dresti was even younger, and life is sweet even when the bitter almonds mingle with the pink and the sour grapes with the purple."

140

"Mark, was he like you?" She had never asked before, but now she felt a compulsion so strong that she had to know. She gazed up at her husband and even savagely scarred he was darkly handsome in the firelight.

He nodded. "Yes, he resembled me. I – I should like to show you his photograph." Mark's lips were clamped tight on his cheroot as he took out his wallet and opened it. He withdrew a small, much-handled photograph and handed it to her.

She studied the dark-haired child whose eyes sparkled with merriment, whose young face mirrored his father's – as it had been before the accident. Ravena gazed for long moments at Dresti's picture, and unbeknown to Mark she was fighting the tears that threatened to spill from her eyes. Now at last she understood a little of what had driven him to seek out the girl close to Rhodri and force her to marry him.

Since the beginning of time, since Eve, since Helen, it had been that way. A woman had to pay because she could assuage bitterness with a certain physical sweetness, and as she returned the photograph to Mark and their hands touched she was reminded again of how alone they were in the shepherd's hut.

"The storm seems to be dying away," she said, but even as she spoke thunder battered the door and soot fell down the chimney and sizzled wetly. She smiled nervously and gave a little shrug, a habit she was picking up from these tough, complex, fatalistic people among whom she had come to live.

"You are tired," Mark said. "You must try and get a few hours' sleep." He took the candle, which had burned very low, and played its fluttering light over the bench on which the shepherd probably slept when he was here to guard his flock. Now he would be high in the hills, where the hot sun of summer had not yet burned the verdure.

"This sleeping bench is rough but quite clean," said Mark.

"What about you?" She did not rise from the stool. "Mark, I'm perfectly comfortable here by the fire –"

"The kindling is almost gone," he said. "When the fire dies, the hut will grow cold, and I prefer that you wrap yourself up on this bench. Come," he held out a hand to her.

"You can hardly sit on this stool," she said hesitantly. "It's so low and you're so tall –"

"I shall be all right." The candleflame illumined his sardonic smile. "Women have a gift for worrying."

"We – we could share the bench." She blushed as if she were still a bride. "You can't roam about the hut all night, Mark. I'd get no sleep at all if I knew you were unable to rest."

"Is it yourself you are thinking of?" He was laughing at her, and suddenly he towered over the low stool on which she sat and lifted her from it with one arm. "I did not suggest sharing the bench with you in case you took alarm – even yet you are nervous of my touch."

He tucked her feet into the sheepskin and made up the fire with the last of the kindling. By now the candle had burned out and it was by the glow of the fire that he came to Ravena and sat down beside her curled-up figure. He drew her against his shoulder and they watched the fire flickering lower and lower.

The sounds of storm faded away, everything became bemused as Ravena sank into the forgetfulness of sleep against the broad shoulder of her husband.

They passed a strange night, and it was around dawn when Ravena awoke to find herself in Mark's arms, her face distractingly close to the warmth of his throat. Still half dreaming, she thought they were together in the Knight's Tower, but as she stirred and looked around she saw the grey light of dawn on the walls of the shepherd's hut and on the dead ashes of the fire.

She let her gaze drift back to Mark, who had fallen asleep with his shoulders against the wall, but whose arms, as the coldness of night had crept into the hut, had pulled her close to him, giving and receiving warmth in an embrace she had not been aware of.

Now she was very aware of how unguarded a man was in the grip of sleep. His hair was ruffled, his chin was blue and unshaven. Such a forceful chin, such well-moulded lips, and cheekbones that held hollows beneath them. His terrible scars could not be transferred to his child, only the unflawed features, the pride and the passion ...

He stirred and she quickly lowered her lashes and felt his arms tighten about her as he began to awaken. He gave a sleepy groan and turned his face so that he nuzzled her. "*Carissima*," he whispered. He had never used the term to her before; it was so caressing, so intimate, that she knew him to be in that half-dreaming state that precedes full awakening.

"*Carissima*." It was an endearment a man used to a woman he loved ... in this unguarded moment Mark thought he held again the lovely Sardinian girl he had loved and lost!

His dark eyes opened, he looked at Ravena, and at once the guarded look sprang into them. He was aware of their surroundings at once and quickly releasing her, he sprang to his feet and stamped the life back into his legs.

"*Dio mio*, what a cheerless place this is in daylight. Come, Ravena! The rain has stopped and it's time we went home."

He swung her off the bench and she stood stretching her arms and running her hands through her untidy hair. "I feel a mess!" she exclaimed.

He ran his eyes over her and a grin quirked his lips. "You look as if you had spent a disreputable night on the tiles, *madame*."

"You should see yourself, sir!" She preceded him out of the hut into the freshness of the morning air. Tiny flames of pink were flickering in the sky and the birds were chirping in the damp trees. They walked through the wet grass and found the car bejewelled by raindrops. Mark wiped the outside of the windscreen before climbing in beside Ravena, and soon they were flashing along through the early morning sunshine.

Tangy scents left by the storm wafted in through the windows. Wild flowers had bloomed on the slopes overnight, and sunrise and sea merged to make a wonderful living picture. Ravena smiled her consent when Mark asked if she would like him to lower the roof of the car. She caught her breath at the hair-tossing rush of the wind ... oh, this early morning ride was worth that strange night shared in the smoky hut, on that hard sleeping bench!

The mountains were misted with a touch of gold. There was a sound of trickling water from hidden falls, poppies splashed the grass and wild mint scented the air. Everything was idyllic, and then they swept round a corner of the upwinding road and Mark's reaction was swift as they almost ran into an enormous uprooted tree that lay sprawled half across the road.

He braked and stopped the car, for it could be seen at once that in order to navigate the car around the tree, torn from the hillside, he must drive close to the edge of the precipitous road.

He leant across Ravena and opened the door beside her. "Please go ahead of me on foot," he said. "I am not driving past that fallen tree with a passenger."

"But, Mark—"

"We won't argue about it." He gave her a fairly gentle push out of the car. "Walk round the tree and wait for me a few yards up the road."

"You are the bossiest man," she said, but she did as she was told. Mark could never forget that other car crash . . . the risks he took by himself he would never take with anyone else.

As she walked around the fallen tree she saw how narrow was the space which Mark must navigate. Her heart leapt into her throat. She wanted to run back to him and beg him not to risk his neck. He could park the car; lock it and leave it on the mountain road for Stelio to collect, but even as she started to go back to him, he started the engine and the Lotus caught the sun on its bonnet as it came towards the margin of road between the sprawled branches of the big tree and the sheer edge of the cliff.

Ravena stood as if sculptured; only her red hair blew in the wind and she hardly seemed to breathe as the car swept the edge of the road and could so easily have plunged all the way down that precipice. Then it drew up beside her and Mark was holding open the door and looking at her with a quizzical question in his eyes.

"Jump in!" he said.

She stood and stared at him. He couldn't care for a soul on earth if he could blithely risk his neck in that way, and sudden anger shook her from head to foot.

"Why drag me into your life?" she demanded. "If you want to be with your ghosts, why couldn't you leave me with my guardian? He cared for me!"

"Ravena –"

She started away from the car and began to run anywhere, she didn't care. She heard behind her the sound of pursuing footfalls and there was a sob in her throat as Mark caught up with her and took hold of her.

"Ravena, I am sorry I frightened you!"

"Y-you didn't frighten me," she threw back at him. "You showed me what an empty farce our marriage is. It can never be anything else! There's no love, no sympathy, nothing but the memories you live with! Oh, why didn't you leave me alone? Do you know, Mark, what you've done to me? Do you care?" She shook her head and her hair caught the sun and seemed alight, but her eyes were lost in shadows. "I saw just now how much you care and I'll never forgive you! Never!"

She broke away from him and returned to the car of her own accord. She slid into her seat, and the morning seemed drained of its earlier beauty. She no longer heard the birds or saw how passionately blue was the sky, how silver the far-down ocean.

She didn't look at Mark as he took the seat beside her and started the car. Her profile was cool and distant, her lips no longer trembled. An icy reserve had descended upon her. She didn't want to speak or be spoken to, and Mark respected her silence as they drove on to the house of the cypress.

The days that followed felt curiously empty. Stelio no longer came to the house and during the day Ravena would take a stroll to the hilltop village, or laze about on the beach. She received a letter from Guardy and replied to it in length. She described Castelmonte in detail, but was reticent about her life with Mark. Even in a letter she could not pretend that she was radiantly happy, and she hoped Guardy would put her reticence down to her natural shyness. At the close of the letter she sent her regards to Rhodri. She couldn't bring herself to write to him, not after that unfinished letter she had let fall into Mark's hands.

He had not referred to it again, but she knew how often he must have read it before burning it, to be able to quote so exactly words she had written and half forgotten. *Those hours with you.* How could she ever convince Mark that talk alone had filled those hours; that the only kiss she and Rhodri had exchanged had been on the platform of the railway station.

She made her way to the village to post her letter and on her way back she passed a doorway in which a dark-shawled woman was making lace. Ravena paused to admire the lace and asked in her much improved Italian if she might buy some. The woman invited her into the house to take a look at samples of her workmanship and Ravena bought a lovely collar and a pair of matching cuffs.

The woman said her name was Virtuella and with a grave smile she asked Ravena to stay and have a cup of coffee with her. That rocky climb to the village had made Ravena feel thirsty and she sat down at the table, which was covered by a blue silk shawl, and watched as Virtuella bustled about her tiny kitchen. Honeycakes were placed on the table and Ravena accepted one and found it delicious.

This was the first time she had been inside one of the square-built houses, with a flight of blue-painted stairs leading to this room, and one other, above the lower part in which Virtuella kept the mule on which she rode to the city to sell her lace.

This small room was spotlessly clean and the walls were blue-washed. In a niche stood a Madonna and Child, both with very blue eyes, and there were flowers in pots and a thin, colourful rug on the floor. A curtained alcove was the bedroom.

Virtuella poured the coffee and said gravely that she was a widow.

"You are all alone?" Ravena's glance found the photograph of a dark-faced young man on the mantel-piece.

"That is my son Marcu." The widow crossed herself as if to chase away a demon. "He is a bad one who never comes to see his mother. He got into the wrong company – the *briganti*."

"I am sorry." Ravena meant it, for it seemed so sad that this nice woman should bring up a son and see him go wrong. When a woman had a child she had such hopes for him, and such a lot of love.

Virtuella sat down at the other side of the table and stirred her coffee. "Marcu left home when he was eighteen," she sighed. "He wanted too many things which I could not give him, and he lost patience with being a shepherd. To be Sardinian, *signora*, is to expect a lot of hard work in one's life. Here in the village things were even harder before the *padrone*, your husband, had water laid on for us, and paid for a city teacher to come and educate the children. He is a good man."

148

Ravena sipped her coffee, which had chicory in it, and thought it premature to mention that Mark had plans to bring electricity to the village. He had told her of his plan one morning as they cantered across the land he loved. He didn't want to see the island and the people spoiled by the commercial values that seemed prevalent elsewhere, but they toiled hard and deserved some of the comforts of modern living. He had been in touch with the authorities and if he was willing to put up half the cost of the project, they would meet him half-way. He was more than willing and Ravena knew that the scheme would be realized. Mark always saw to the finish whatever he started!

"You will eat another cake, *signora*?" Virtuella held out the plate and Ravena didn't say no to another crunchy honey-cake.

"*Grazie*. You must tell me how to make these. I used to do a lot of cooking before my marriage and I must try my hand again." Ravena's smile was a little wry. "We had no servants, you see. We were quite poor. I often long to invade the kitchen at the Casa, but Donna Jocasta runs things and I don't like to – to upset her."

Virtuella gazed at Ravena as if surprised by this latter statement, then she said slowly: "You are different from the Signora Donata – she always ran things! And never did she buy lace from me for a dress. Her dresses were bought in Rome – so smart and *bellissima* did she always look."

"I have seen her portrait," Ravena said quietly. "She was exquisite to look at."

"She looked the great lady," said Virtuella.

Ravena detected an ironic note in Virtuella's voice and her own glance was inquiring.

"A lady is like yourself." Virtuella opened a painted cigar-box that stood on the table and took from it a pack of cards. "You don't look down on anyone, *signora*."

"Did Donata do that?"

"After she caught and married the young *padrone*. He was so handsome." Virtuella shuffled the cards. "There was not a man from here to Sicily to hold a candle to him and it was a feather in a girl's cap to catch such an *hombre de amor*."

"That is Spanish," Ravena said in almost a whisper. "A man to love!"

"All the girls would watch and sigh after him. He was like a young prince." Virtuella began to lay out the cards face downward. "Now the *signor padrone* is more of a man than ever. He has suffered and it makes or breaks a man, or a woman. *Signora*, you would like me to read the cards for you?"

"You mean," Ravena's heart beat fast, "you want to read my fortune?"

Virtuella inclined her head and she looked rather like a gipsy with her swarthy, sun-lined skin and her dark head-shawl; her eyes upon Ravena's face were keen, knowing, friendly. "You are not afraid of what the cards might reveal? Or perhaps you are sceptical?"

"No." Ravena shook her head and a finger of sunshine stroked her bright hair. "I'm a Celt – that means I don't laugh at magic, that I believe there are people who are clairvoyant."

"Then turn face upward any three of the cards I have laid out."

Ravena did so and her hostess studied the cards intently. It was very quiet in the house, the only sounds came from the cicadas on the roof, and every now and again the mule below kicked his stall as if bored with his own company.

"Ah, there is a festivity in store for you, *signora*. Do you see, there is a clown on your first card, and he laughs." Virtuella tapped it with her finger, for the cards had pictures on them and were not ordinary playing-cards. "Yes, a festival, a good time for you."

"Perhaps it's the Festival of Madre Rosaria," Ravena smiled. "We are going."

"You and the *signor*?"

"Yes. He wishes to go this year."

Virtuella nodded, and then her dark eyes became fixed on the third card, as if the second one held little of significance. "A bird with black wings," she murmured. "Ah, that is an omen, *signora*! It could mean –"

There she paused and scanned Ravena's face.

"What could it mean?" Ravena's finger gripped the fringe of the table covering. "Please tell me!"

"A – a time not quite happy." Virtuella shuffled the cards together. "Bad news, perhaps – ah, but this is just a game and you must not take it too much to heart."

"No," Ravena said, but she looked pensive, troubled as she rose to her feet. "I must be getting home. Thank you for selling me the lace collar and cuffs. I know they'll look lovely on my green dress –"

All the way home to the Casa Ravena's thoughts were on the card reading. She wanted to believe it was just a game, but as she neared home and the sun began to slant the shadows of the cypress trees, a lone bird flew across the sky and for a moment was etched darkly against the rose-gold and the tinges of lavender.

A lone, dark bird, just like the one on the card she had turned up!

A breeze stirred through the foliage of the cypresses

as she entered the courtyard of the house, it touched her skin like a cold finger ... and then she saw Mark standing in the shadow of one of the alcoves smoking a cheroot. Ravena hastened across to him, clutching the little package that held the lace collar and cuffs.

"Hullo!" She wanted him to put his arm around her, to have his masculine warmth dispel the coldness of a moment ago. But she had been cold towards him for days running and he didn't make any attempt to touch her.

"Where have you been?" he asked casually.

"To the village. I – I bought some lace." Something was gripping and hurting her throat ... he seemed so distant and unaware of her need for comfort. "From a terribly nice woman named Virtuella. I stayed and had coffee with her."

"Good," he said, tapping the ash from his cheroot. "I am glad you are making a few friends."

She lowered her eyes, for tears had come into them. She went indoors and across the hall to the stairs, and never had the house of the cypress seemed so alien, and so alone among the mountains.

CHAPTER EIGHT

THE vines hung heavy with ripening grapes, but their juice was bittersweet on Ravena's tongue, for they were not yet ready for pressing. The figs had grown plump on the trees, and the scent from the lemon groves was rich and tangy. Everything was so rich with life that it was a relief to Ravena to escape to the *grotta*, just like a sunken garden with its cool green plants and its coolly trickling fountain.

There she would read a book, or dabble her fingers in the fountain and ponder about the future. Sometimes it would be hours before her sanctuary was invaded by a servant who came to tell her lunch was ready, or there was a visitor for tea.

When the wives of Mark's business associates came to call, she would have to make a dash upstairs to change her lounging clothes for a formal dress. The leaf-green linen that looked charming since she had sewn on the lace collar and cuffs. Or the champagne pink that made her look almost too young to be the wife of Mark di Curzio.

She was aware that these smart women from the city and the coast were critical of her because she seemed so unworldly. She knew, despite her air of innocence, that they envied her youth and the wonderful red hair of her Celtic heritage. They hinted that Mark must be an overwhelming man for her to manage.

"I don't attempt to manage Mark," she laughed. "It would be like the kitten trying to tame the tiger."

"Does he ever talk about Donata?" she was asked. "Such a beauty – and not in the least kittenish."

Donna Jocasta was never present at these "inquisitorials", as Ravena called them in the privacy of her thoughts, but she liked to hear what had been said and now and again Ravena was invited to take a glass of wine with *la nonna* in her own wing of the house.

Long velvet curtains closed out half the sunlight, and *la nonna* sat with her tiny feet propped on a footstool and dipped sponge fingers in her glass of wine while she listened to a resumé of yesterday's gossip. All the time her eyes were fixed on Ravena as she sat in one of the overstuffed chairs, and at last, to escape those searching, jetty eyes, Ravena would stare down into her wine, or at the ornaments on every available space, including the surface of the piano.

"Baptista plays to me sometimes." *La nonna* gestured at her companion, who sat sewing in a far corner of the *sala*. "I enjoy a little music – do you play, child?"

"Yes." Ravena had learned on the upright piano at Ravenhall, and she had often played old Welsh songs to Guardy while the rain streamed down outside and the room grew dusky.

"*Bene.*" *La nonna* clapped her hands. "You will play for me!"

Ravena sat down at the inlaid piano and made herself feel so homesick with well-remembered tunes that it was a relief to escape at last from the *sala*.

Baptista glanced up from her sewing and gave her a rather jealous look. Ravena met the woman's eyes and felt choked by the stuffy, high-necked dress she wore, and by the smell of dust on the ornaments, the old-fashioned perfume and sweet wine. She had a sudden longing to take out her colt and have a canter.

She hastened to her room and changed into riding trousers and a shirt, and bundled her hair beneath the brim of a slouch hat. Ten minutes later she was in the saddle and riding off into the sunshine that still lingered.

These were long, hot days, but there was always a wind blowing across the grassy plateau that soared above the sea and it was sheer delight to ride into the tangy wind. Her colt's mane flew proudly and he seemed as happy as she to be out in the open air, and they were cantering along the headland when a sudden gust of wind blew her hat from her head and she had to dismount in order to retrieve it. It had been carried to the edge of the cliffs, where it lodged against a hummock of grass.

Ravena pounced on it, and then instinctively she glanced downwards and saw a man and a girl talking together on the path below. The girl had dark hair that rippled and blew in the breeze. She was talking earnestly to the man and suddenly she flung her arms about his neck and buried her face against his shoulder. He did not repulse her but seemed to draw her closer to him.

The grass grew tall above the couple and Ravena knelt there and stared down frozenly. She would have known the man in any crowd ... on the path with the girl he was unmistakable.

She arose and walked away. She even thought she recognized the girl in Mark's arms ... it was the tanned, bare-footed girl from the *trattoria* where they served freshly caught sardines, and where pomegranates grew rusty-gold on the wall of the garden.

Ravena's colt had his slender neck bent to the grass and when she rested her face against his silky coat he turned his head and gave her a look of animal sympathy, as if her diminished joy in the afternoon was transmitted to him.

Her feeling was not one of anger or shock, she just felt sad ... sad because Mark had made her marry him when he might have been happier, perhaps able to forget the past, with a girl of his own people. A girl born and bred here, who loved the island as he did, who understood the Sards and their complexity, their disturbing charm, their deepness.

She sighed, and her colt sighed with her, and stroking his neck she remounted and turned his head towards the Casa Cipresso. She returned home through the vineyards, and had an excuse later on for not going down to dinner. She said she had been eating the half-ripe grapes and had a slight tummyache.

Mark left his tie undone and came to her bedside. He bent down and felt her forehead with the back of his hand. "You do feel a little feverish," he said. "I have half a mind to send for the doctor –"

"No – please don't, Mark!" She shrank away from his touch. "I shall be all right, but I couldn't face any dinner."

"Perhaps something light on a tray?" he suggested.

She shook her head, for she had no appetite and only wished to be left alone. Mark stared down at her, for the lamp at her bedside made eyelash-shadows on her cheeks, and curled up on her great bed she looked lost, and sad.

"Would you like me to stay with you?" he asked.

"No!" The word broke from her. "No – I shall be all right."

"What is it, Ravena?"

She glanced up at him and he looked rakish with his

tie undone and his hair not yet combed into its usual order. The emotion she had not felt earlier knifed through her and she wanted to scorn his offer to stay with her when his thoughts, his longings must be with that other girl. Tanned and sea-bloomed, with dark-brown eyes that had been raised to him with such hope that afternoon.

"I want to be left alone," she said.

"Because you have been eating sour grapes?"

She winced, for it was as if he read her mind and was being ironic. She turned away from him, but he was not having that and the bed took his weight as he sat down on the side of it. He reached for her and held her with her hair spreading its flame against the white pillows and her eyes burning green against the pallor of her face.

"What are you sulking about?" he demanded. "Has *la nonna* said something to upset you? I had the impression that you were beginning to make friends with her."

"Mark, do I have to account for my every mood? Can't I be left in peace *at all*?"

"You are in a strange mood and it worries me, Ravena."

"I'm sorry I give you cause for concern." She gave him a cold look and wished he would release her from the arms in which he had held that other girl. "I'm not pining away, Mark, so don't let it spoil your dinner."

And then she caught her breath as his hands buried themselves in the cream velvet of her robe, with its fur-edged sleeves falling back from her slender arms. His face came close to her, dark and fire-scarred, and with a look of reproach smouldering in his eyes. *He* dared to reproach her?

"Let me go!" she pleaded. "I – I can't bear to be touched tonight!"

"What is it you hate the most?" he asked quietly. "My scars, or my kisses?"

Again she felt that stab of pain and her mouth shaped a silent cry as it flickered through her body and made her feel boneless in his arms. He released her and she lay unmoving in her velvet robe as he walked from her room into his own and closed the door quietly behind him.

He didn't come in again, and half an hour later a tray was brought to her and on it was a slice of melon, a tenderly cooked lamb chop with broccoli and mashed potatoes, and a glass of delicate white wine.

There was a folded note beside the glass of wine and Ravena felt her fingers shake as she opened it. "*I am called away by a business matter and I hope to return by the week-end, when the Festival of Madre Rosaria takes place. Perhaps by then we will both be in the mood for a festa. Mark.*"

She gazed at the deep, slanting writing, and quite as vividly she saw a dark, tanned girl in his arms, and a strand of dark hair whipped by the wind across his face.

Her fingers slowly crushed his note. Like her, he was finding their marriage an intolerable strain, yet it was he who had enforced it. It was he, despite what he believed about her and Rhodri, who was making it harder to bear.

She ate the food on the tray without tasting it, and later she sat at her window and watched the new moon rising over the cypress trees. A slither of pure silver, with a retinue of stars that shone brightly in the wind washed sky. The night time scents were poignant, and

Ravena wondered as she sat alone whether Mark was alone....

Ravena awoke on the morning of the *festa* with that sense of excitement and hope which is part of being young. For a whole day and a night she would escape from the Casa, and the colour and fervour, and the fun of the festival would be like a holiday.

Mark had returned late the evening before, and she could hear him in the adjoining room, opening a cupboard, dropping a boot ... perhaps in his excitement at the forthcoming day.

She washed behind the screen from head to toe, and her young maid came to help her put on the colourful costume which had belonged to Demelza. The girl was full of the *festa* and who was going, and from her account it seemed as if the entire village was off into the hills that day. Every member of her own family was going in a decorated cart. It looked splendid, with its ribbons and garlands, and the mule would be decked out with rosettes.

"I thought this was a religious festival," Ravena smiled.

"Ah, but yes, *padroncina*. The image of Madre Rosaria will be carried at the head of a torchlight procession and everyone will be blessed by the priest, but there will also be fireworks and roasted meats and music."

"I can see, Rosita, that you can't wait to get there." Ravena adjusted the pea-green silk of her frilled skirt over the flounces of her petticoats. "Is your boy-friend going with you?"

Rosita blushed and lowered her pansy-brown eyes. "Tonio is taking me with him on horseback, the way that most sweethearts go to the *festa*."

"What a charming custom!" Ravena opened her jewel-box to take out her pearl cross to wear against the bodice of her snowy frilled blouse, and she noticed a pair of sparkling earrings which she rarely wore. She took them out of the box and told Rosita to stand still while she adjusted the small glittering hoops to the lobes of her ears.

"*Padroncina*," the girl's blush deepened and her eyes lit up, "for me?"

"Yes. How pretty they look. Now run along and get ready to go with Tonio to the *festa*."

"You are so kind – " the girl caught at Ravena's hand and before she could stop it, the rosy young lips had pressed a kiss to her fingers. "It is a privilege to serve you, *padroncina*."

"Run along and don't keep your young man waiting," Ravena said gently.

The girl shook her head to feel the glittering rings in her ears, then with a happy smile she hastened away, and as Ravena clasped Demelza's cross about her throat she wondered what it felt like to be as carefree as her young maid, off to the *festa* with a boy who loved her.

All was quiet in the adjoining room, so she guessed Mark had gone down to breakfast. She felt a little stab of pain that he had not come in to take a look at her in the lovely costume which he had given her.

She studied her reflection in the long mirror of the wardrobe and was not displeased with her appearance. The pea-green silk and the flounces of cream beneath the hem, which was slightly raised, suited her colouring. Her hair was braided into a glowing coronet, and her neck rose gracefully out of the crisp frills of her blouse. Her eyes shone as green as gems, for despite Mark's neglect of her, she felt excited and was resolved to enjoy every moment of the *festa*.

Would Stelio be there? She missed his teasing and hoped she would see him.

Feeling rather like a girl of an earlier century, she gathered her full skirts into her hands and made her way down the stairs from the Knight's Tower. There wasn't anyone about. The servants had been given the day off and the Casa felt deserted.

Ravena rustled across the hall to the *salottino*, and there was her breakfast, all covered and ready on the table. Coffee, rolls and honey, ample fare for Ravena who wondered, as she drank her coffee, where Mark had got to. Perhaps he was with *la nonna*, who had said sardonically last night that she had enjoyed her share of festivals and her bones were too old to feel at ease on a bed of bracken and thyme, with a bonfire smoking into her eyes.

Because she felt too restless to sit still, Ravena went out to the courtyard where she stood in the sunshine and ate a crisp roll spread with honey. She was wiping her lips when the sound of hoofbeats clattered on the cobbles and Adonis appeared in the courtyard with Mark in the saddle.

The great horse tossed his mane and the muscles rippled beneath the black satin of his coat. Mark wore dark riding breeches and an embroidered waistcoat over a frilled shirt. The brim of his hat made his eyes gleam darkly in its shadow – he looked every inch a Sard – or an arrogant *cavaliere* about to ride out with hawks and hounds.

"*Avanti!*" He held out a hand to her and his teeth flashed against his sun-dark skin. "Everyone will arrive at the *festa* ahead of us if we don't hurry."

Her heart beat fast ... he meant them to ride together to the *festa* ... but only sweethearts, only lovers rode that way.

"Come," he snapped his fingers and his signet ring glittered in the sunshine, "mount on my boot and sit in front of me."

This was not the first time his eyes had drawn her to him, fascinated against her will, and as he bent to her, his knees gripped the saddle and with one powerful movement he lifted her up in front of him. Her cream flounces and pea-green silk were bright against the horse's glossy coat, and she gave a little shiver – strangely close to pleasure – as Mark's strong arm encircled her, holding her safe as the stallion cantered out of the courtyard on to the sunlit road.

Soon they were part of a gay cavalcade making its way with leisure into the mountains to the Chapel of Madre Rosaria. There were mules laden with bundles of bedding and brown, laughing children. There were carts painted orange and blue, their ribbons blowing in the wind, and Arab ponies picking their way up the twisting paths with handsome couples sharing the saddle, clad in brilliant costume, and singing to the accordion music being played in the festive carts.

The scene had a dreamlike quality about it, and Ravena was quiet like a child who dare not speak or move for fear the magic would be dispelled.

She felt Mark looking down at her and she strove not to think of the three days he had been away from her; she clung to the magic of the moment.

She glanced up at Mark, her head draped against the hot sun by the lace scarf beneath which her hair shimmered like fire under frost. "It's wonderful, isn't it?" she said. "Everyone for miles around must be on their way to the Chapel – look at those four little boys on that mule, and that woman walking like a Bedouin with a basket of food on her head. Mark, our food! We've forgotten to bring it!"

He laughed, and he seemed so carefree and gay that she couldn't help but wonder who had put that gleam in his eyes. "I have provided a pair of hogs for the feast this evening, and when we halt for lunch there will be so many of these good people pressing pies and cheese and fruit upon us that we won't know how to eat all they give us."

His eyes seemed to deepen and darken as he gazed down at Ravena. "I have not attended the *festa* for some time, and I fear we will be overwhelmed by kindness and goodwill."

Even as he spoke a woman leant from one of the beribboned carts and called out happily: "It is good that we have our *padrone* and his lady with us this year. May the blessing of Madre Rosaria be upon both of you!"

"And upon you, *signora*, and your good husband and little ones." Ravena felt Mark's arm tighten about her as he replied, and looking up at him she saw in his face that dark beauty Virtuella had spoken about the day she had bought the lace.

"He was like a prince – an *hombre de amor*," she had said.

Today, in the local Sard costume, with his eyes taking pleasure in the cavalcade, the children, all the sunlit, savage beauty of the mountains, he was again like a prince. And as the scented wind blew the ends of her lacy scarf against his face, she was reminded of their wedding day and that moment outside the church when the wind had blown her veil across his face and hidden his scars.

She had glimpsed a man unravaged by the burning need to revenge himself. She glimpsed that man again, and she lifted her hand and pressed his scarred hand to her breast, where the cross of Demelza was lost among the frills of her blouse. It was a gesture of compassion, as if she sought to ease the memory of pain from the bones and sinews and sunbrowned skin of his hand.

They didn't speak again until everyone halted for lunch, halfway up the mountains, and as soon as Mark lifted her from the back of his horse they were surrounded by the members of a large family and made captives of their hospitality.

It was fun to picnic in the long grass, with the thyme blowing, and the small ones chasing hawk-moths from flower to wild flower. Never had country bread and thick slices of ham tasted so good, spiced by dark, luscious olives and washed down with red wine. Everyone took a short siesta, or sang lazily as the musicians played their guitars, and when the time came to move on the sweet, heavy fragrances clung to Ravena's senses, and to her skirts and her skin as she walked with Mark to where Adonis grazed in the grass beside a mountain stream.

She brushed the silky down of blue thistles from her skirts and smiled lazily at Mark. The sunlight was in her hair, warm on the soft skin of her half-bared shoulders. Her eyes were a hazy, lazy green, and Mark's hands felt a little cruel as he took her around the waist to lift her on to the horse.

"*Mark!*" she gasped.

"You little witch!" His teeth were bone-white against his taut, sun-dark skin. "Such eyes, the colour of leaves, and danger, and Venetian glass. You might break in my grip . . . or turn to a statue."

And she gasped again as he pulled her away from the

horse and around a great rock that loomed by the stream. There he kissed her in the thyme and wild-growing poppies, and it was the most pagan thing she had ever known. It startled and thrilled her, and her lips returned the pressure of his and were like poppy petals when Mark let her go.

"Oh – " she said, and laid an arm across her eyes. The thyme was crushed beneath them, and Mark leant upon an elbow and looked at her, his black hair tousled above eyes in which the youth had come savagely alive.

"For the first time," he murmured, "you kissed me as a woman should. But if you ever kissed another man like that, Ravena, I would choke you with your lovely hair."

He unbraided her hair and wound the fiery strands about her slim, creamy throat. "Well, Ravena, did you ever kiss Rhodri Brenin like that?"

"Don't, Mark," she pleaded, "not today. Please forget Rhodri, and I'll forget about that girl – "

There she broke off as his eyes narrowed and sharpened. "What girl do you mean?"

"*You know*." She broke free of his hand on her shoulder and scrambled to her feet. "Everyone is leaving–we had better go with them – "

She cast one look at his face, and his dark frown, and the sun seemed to go cold for her. As he took a step towards her, she caught at her pea-green skirts and fled round the big rock to where Adonis stood, and where other people were packing up the picnic and preparing for the second half of the trek to the Chapel – so high in the hills, they said, that the wind rang the bells.

Almost without thinking she ran to the horse and put her foot in the stirrup –

"*Ravena!*" The cry was urgent, but she thought it angry, and she caught at Adonis' mane to assist herself into the saddle. People turned to look at her, pausing to strap a food basket or to lift a child into a cart, and looks of consternation appeared on their faces as the great horse reared up on his hind legs, unseating the girl and throwing her backwards, one foot caught in the stirrup, her bright hair trailing the ground.

Even as cries of alarm broke out, Mark bounded across to the horse, the murderous lash of the hooves right above him as he wrenched at the bridle and forced Adonis to calm down. A youth leapt forward and grabbed hold of Ravena, who was dazed and bitting her lips with pain.

Amidst a babble of voices, Mark released her foot from the stirrup and she couldn't suppress a cry as he felt her ankle, which was badly wrenched and bruised. Brandy stung her lips, and her eyes were fixed on the lividity of Mark's scars as her ankle was bound tightly with strips of cloth which someone dipped in vinegar and cold water from the nearby stream.

"I will take you home," Mark said, and with a brusque hand he stroked the dishevelled hair back from her pale face.

"No," she caught at his arm, "I want to go to the *festa*."

"*Buon festa*," he growled, while sympathetic faces peered over his shoulder, and a woman murmured that the *padroncina* was welcome to ride with her and her children in the family cart.

"Please let me, Mark." Ravena forced a smile to shaky lips. "And do take that expression *terribilita* off your face – you frighten me more than Adonis did."

"I suppose you realize that you could have been trampled?" he said through his teeth. "What were you trying to do – run away from me again?"

She bit her lip. "Mark, we're holding everyone up – "

"Were you?" he insisted.

"If you want to hear me say yes, then it's yes." Her green eyes warred with his. "Anything to get moving."

"One of these days, Ravena, I shall spank you," he said, and someone in the crowd understood the English word and gave a chuckle. That fat chuckle seemed to break the tension, and Mark lifted her up in his arms and carried her to a beribboned cart in which several curly heads peered over the side.

"Come, make room for the *signora*." Their mother shooed them into a bunch, and provided a folded blanket for Ravena to sit on. "There, rest your foot on this basket, *signora*."

"*Grazie*, you are more than kind." Ravena smiled at the four tots, stricken with shyness on the seat at the other side of the cart. The little girl was staring at Mark's face, and after a few words to Ravena he turned and strode over to where Adonis stood with his head down. Ravena watched him swing into the saddle, and when she looked across the cart she saw the little girl lift a hand to her cheek and stroke it. Her enormous eyes questioned Ravena.

"The *signor* is my husband," she said gently. "His face was hurt in a fire."

"Poor face," said the child, and Ravena had to look away as tears stung and burned in her eyes. *Oh, Mark, I wish I understood what holds us together – what is driving us apart.*

The beribboned mule cart wended its way up the twisting paths to the Chapel of Madre Rosaria, and tinges of pink were in the sky when they heard the bells ringing in the whitewashed tower of the chapel.

"We are almost there!"

The shyness of the four children had long since evaporated and they clustered around Ravena, though their mother kept turning from the driving seat to tell them to mind the *padroncina*'s bandaged ankle. Her husband dozed in the seat beside her, a brown and craggy farmer, sleeping, said his wife, because he worked so hard all the year round that a holiday always took him that way.

"Lazybones," she prodded him. "Wake and hear the bells – we are almost there at the Chapel."

And as they came in sight of the roughcast walls, the conical tower and wide-flung doors, Ravena saw a black horse on the hill outlined against the sunset. The rider sat very still in the saddle, and there was a loneliness about him; an air of detachment from the bustle and chatter and welcoming peal of the bells.

Of what was he thinking as he sat there? Ravena watched him and wondered if he was thinking of the last time he had attended the festival ... or of the first time he had attended it with Donata. They would have shared his saddle all the way up the mountains, until they reached the chapel. And to the music of the bells he might have whispered: "I love you, Donata ... I will always love you."

Then suddenly he turned his horse's head and cantered towards the cart, which had come to a halt on the hillside. "Welcome to the Chapel of Madre Rosaria," he called out above the happy din. "Later we will go in and light candles – tell me, how is the ankle?"

"Stiff," she admitted, "but I can hobble."

He leapt from the back of his horse and came to assist her from the cart. "Hullo!" said a quiet little voice.

He glanced down and there was a very small girl with

very large eyes peeping round Ravena's silk skirts. She smiled at him, and after a moment he smiled back.

"I fear I must take this lady away with me," he said.

"Oh?" The smile quivered on the child's lips.

"You see, little one," he bent from his great height and touched gently the soft young cheek, "I shall have no one with whom to share the *festa*. I shall be all alone when they let off the fireworks."

"You have no children, *signore*?"

"No, *carina*, I have no children, but the *signora* is my wife and I would like to share the fireworks with her — may I?"

The little girl smiled and nodded and let go of the bunch of pea-green skirt she was clasping. Mark lifted Ravena from the cart and when she looked at him she found that his smile had faded to sombreness. It was inevitable, of course, that a charming child should remind him of his own lost child; when he waved to the little one, that night-dark look was back in his eyes.

"Come, we must find a nook of our own for the night and lay our bed-roll there to let others see it has been claimed." He glanced down into her eyes as he carried her. "You realized that we would be spending tonight in the hills?"

She nodded, and saw bonfires and lanterns beginning to spring to life in the dusk. The bells pealed on and on, echoing over the mountains, touching the heart with a sense of magic. Soon a thousand candles would bloom in the dim interior of the Chapel, and there would be a torchlight procession, in which the image of Madre Rosaria would be carried shoulder-high for all to see, then fireworks would light the sky and there would be feasting and music.

It was exciting and elemental ... these hills reached

for the stars, and there would be stars in her eyes when she slept in the bracken tonight with the man whose every look and action both mystified and disturbed her.

She felt the hard bone and sinew of his shoulder under her hand, and she wondered if the girl from the *trattoria* was at the festival.

CHAPTER NINE

FIREWORKS soared and burst and showered coloured light upon the eager upraised faces. Some of the fireworks were like wheels of fire, others burst into gold and emerald sprays, and for brief moments they outshone the stars.

Over glowing fires of charçoal the roasting hogs turned on iron spits, crackling juicily, and when fat fell into the fire there were little bursts of flame that lit the eyes and gleamed on the sweating faces of the men who presided over the barbecues. There mingled with the smell of the pork the tang of almonds roasting in pans on the edges of the fires.

Children dashed about clutching balloons, and there was a peddler selling trinkets, and another selling costumed dolls, while a raven perched on the shoulder of a gipsy and plucked fortune cards from a tambourine for laughing young couples.

Ravena was so absorbed by everything that she almost forgot her aching ankle. She wore a traditional costume that made her feel like those laughing girls; the arm of a Sard in frilled shirt, red sash and dark breeches was around her waist. She was confused by her own sense of happiness, and she clung to it as those excited children clung to their coloured balloons that might catch a spark at any moment and go pop.

"Will you have a trinket, a doll, or a glimpse into the future?" Mark asked. "You can have all three if you wish."

"I'm not one for trinkets, and I've had my fortune

told." She smiled hesitantly. "I think I should like a doll."

Mark beckoned the peddler so Ravena wouldn't have to limp through the crowd on her sore ankle, and she chose a doll clad in a scarlet frilled dress, an embroidered bolero, and with a tiny square of lace over her plaits. "The one in pink also." Mark picked it out and handed it to Ravena. "For the little girl with the big eyes," he smiled. "With luck we will see her again."

Ravena was pleased that he should remember her little friend of the beribboned cart, and she admired the dolls as Mark paid for them. Her heart beat fast and she told herself it was the excitement of the *festa* that made her pulses race; the rare memory of entering the chapel with Mark and lighting candles in front of the baroque altar, where the cluster of tiny flames lit up the image of Madre Rosaria – the saint of mothers to the people of the hills.

Ravena had not dared to look at Mark as people whispered, "*Madonnina*," and crossed themselves. Always ... unforgettable, was the memory of what he had said to her at Ravenhall. "You will give back what I have lost ... you will give me a son."

"Who told your fortune?" Mark's arm was around her, strong and supporting, as they made their way to where a lantern-lit puppet-show was in progress, with rows of children seated on benches, their dark, shining eyes fixed in wonderment on the life-like puppets.

"It was a woman who lives in the village. She makes lace and has the wonderful name of Virtuella."

"Virtuella?" He spoke the name thoughtfully. "Widow with one son, who has left home and got into bad company."

172

"Can't you do something about that, Mark?" Ravena glanced up eagerly. "Virtuella is a good, hard-working woman and she is desperately worried about her son."

"You must understand that before anyone could help Marcu, he would have to leave the gang he has joined and be taken into custody for a while. The trouble is, Ravena," a grave note came into Mark's voice, "what we want from other people is not always what they are prepared to give. I tried the other day to explain that – why, look, there is the little girl with the pink ribbons in her hair!"

She was gazing rapturously at the puppets, her small hands clasping and unclasping as one of the puppets chased round and round after a donkey, who kept kicking up a back leg and letting out a derisive hee-haw.

"How children love to watch puppets," Mark murmured.

Ravena caught the sadness in his voice and she guessed that two years ago he had stood here with his small son, who had laughed as these children laughed; whose eyes had shone with the same truth and happiness.

"Give the child the doll," he added, and he turned away and a match flared as he lit a cheroot. The smoke veiled the expression in his eyes as they walked away together from the sound of young laughter, and lost was the thread of conversation regarding Virtuella and her son.

The evening wore on, and after the fireworks came the carving up of roasted hogs. Everyone sat in groups round the bonfires and ate the crisp pork with hunk of bread broken off the great halter-shaped loaves.

The red wine circulated, and old Sardinian songs were played on the concertinas and the mandolins.

It was an hour to be treasured, with the shadows held at bay beyond the firelight. The country food tasted good, the wine left a tingle in the veins, and a man's shoulder was comfortable to lean against while the brushwood and almond shells crackled together and the tips of the flames played over faces with a strength, a beauty, a certain element of gravity.

Her own hair reflected the glow of the fire; her eyes shone green as she listened to a Sardinian song about a shepherd in love. It pleased her that her grasp of the local dialect had grown so keen that she could understand the words. *"Life makes me cry, and laugh, and sigh. I love it all – and you I love beyond all else."*

Something made her look at Mark as the music and the words died away. She thought she saw a flash of tenderness in his eyes, and then she knew the cause as a slim figure stepped suddenly into the firelight. Dark-haired, bare-footed, a tambourine in hand. The girl from the *trattoria*, smiling round at everyone, and then running on bare brown feet until her red skirts flared out and touched the ground in front of Mark and his wife.

Her smile, seen close to, had a certain desperation about it. *"Padrone?"* she said, and there was an imploring note in the word, her dark eyes held his as she arose and began her tambourine dance.

Ravena sat tense against Mark's shoulder. She hardly knew how she sat through the dance ... she wanted to jump to her feet and run away. But her ankle would allow her to hobble only a few yards, and in her pride she would not be put to such undignified flight by the girl who danced for her husband alone.

She thought the dance would never end, for now it was unbearable to sit so close to Mark that her hair brushed his chin, and the hard warmth of his shoulder penetrated the silk of her blouse. The tambourine shook and the girl's shadow was everywhere in the firelight ... when at last she melted away, her shadow remained and cast a gloom over Ravena that she couldn't shake off.

People began to yawn and drift off to the shake-downs in the brushwood or the carts. "It has been good." They smiled and kissed each other on the cheeks. "A happy *festa*."

Ravena felt Mark's hands on her shoulders. She glanced up wildly as he drew her against him. His mouth touched hers gently, but she pulled away without returning the kiss.

"It is customary." A cold note came into his voice. "Has the *festa* not been a happy one for you?"

"I – I've had quite a nice time," she said.

"A nice time?" He smiled mockingly. "My dear, when will you learn to be like us and to feel passionately about something? To look fierce enough to pluck the earrings from your ears – should another girl try to steal your lover."

"I'm not wearing earrings," she said coldly, " and the other girl is welcome to what she can steal." Ravena swung away from him with a rustle of pea-green silk, but her dignity was spoiled by her wretched ankle. It almost gave way beneath her and she had to accept Mark's support to their bed among the brushwood.

It was a velvety southern night, brilliant with starlight, and though Ravena had slept out in the open on camping trips with school friends, tonight was not quite the same. She could hear the wind singing through the mountain trees, and she would share with Mark the sheepskin-lined rug which he had spread over the tangy bracken. It was so enormous that it would enwrap them comfortably against the chill in the mountain air.

"That bandage about your ankle should be loosened slightly," he said. "Sit on this fallen tree and I'll see to it for you."

It was never wise to argue with Mark, so she did as she was told and felt the strong touch of his fingers as he unwound the strip of linen and readjusted it so that her leg wouldn't go numb while she slept.

"There, is that comfortable?"

"Fine, thank you."

He stood up and leaned against a tree and after a second a match flared, lighting up his face as he lit a cheroot. His eyes rested upon her, narrowed in thought.

"You said something – just before your mishap – that I had forgotten until now. You referred to a girl –"

"Mark," her throat hurt as she spoke his name, "this is hardly the time and the place to discuss the subject. I'm tired – there are other people nearby."

"Of course, but just answer me this, Ravena. Don't you like to think of me with someone else?"

The question struck her as infinitely cruel. "If you want someone else, then let me go." She stood up and faced him in the blazing starlight. "Don't keep me with you, Mark – you know there can be no happiness for us – as things are."

She turned away and went to lie down on the sheepskin rug. The stars shone in her eyes and the drifting aroma of a cheroot was in her nostrils. She hoped she would fall asleep before he joined her, but tired out as she was by the mixed pleasures and pains of this *festa* day, she still lay wakeful when the bracken crackled beneath his approaching tread.

She stiffened, her whole body tensed against his touch as he lay down beside her and threw the rug over them. Her heart beat loudly as she waited for his warm arm to enclose her. It was something he did automatically, before falling asleep, as if the long-ago habit of cuddling something in sleep still clung to him. But tonight he lay withdrawn from her, staring up at the stars.

An owl hooted among the trees. A child cried plaintively and the sound of the mother's voice soothed away his tears. Ravena listened and pillowed her cheek against the warm sheepskin ... soon she slept, and night wrapped the mountains and the whitewashed belltower of the Chapel of Madre Rosaria.

They awoke early and rolled up their bedding and departed for home while the dew still sparkled on the tall grass and the silvery leaves of the olive-trees. Ravena had the feeling that Mark was impatient to get away from the mountains – perhaps to see the dark-haired girl again.

They didn't speak, and only the birds and the sound of Adonis' hooves broke the silence as they galloped homewards. Ravena's pea-green finery was crushed, and her hair blew in the wind, whipping across Mark's throat.

Suddenly she laughed, and there was a mixture of sweet and bitter in the sound ... a feeling that she was saying good-bye to all this.

"Why do you laugh?"

She glanced up at him and it seemed to her that his face was unusually grim and determined, as if he had made a decision about something and that imparting it to her would not be pleasant.

"I feel like a Sabine across your saddlebow." The wind tossed her hair, and they seemed the only two people in the mountains this morning, as if all the world had left them alone. Nothing will ever be like this again, she thought. I shall never feel so alive, so aware of just being a woman with a man. In the strangest way I have touched the heights when I thought only to touch the depths. Mark ... oh, Mark, if I could only know your heart as I know your face and your kiss!

They arrived home just after noon, and Ravena was glad to get to her room, to wash all over and change into something light and floating.

She ate alone, and spent the afternoon in welcome solitude. She felt instinctively that Mark stayed away from her because he had something to say that was of intense importance to their future together, and later she dressed in a cool linen dress and went down stairs to await him in the *grotta*.

It was a peaceful room, with its green shadows and tinkling fountain and lazy gold fish twirling the water-lily leaves. Here she sought calmness of heart and mind ... and here Mark came to her.

He looked a different man in his grey lounge suit. Stern, tall, aloof – not at all the picturesque Sard who had carried her off to the *festa* on his great horse.

"How is your ankle?" His eyes dwelt on her foot, resting on a little stool.

"Bruised, but I'll live. Won't you sit down, Mark? You unnerve me, towering over me." She smiled, but felt the effort of it, and the aching in her throat.

He sat down in one of the wickerwork chairs and

sought in his pocket for his cheroot-case. "May I smoke?"

"Of course," she said. " You know I like the smell of them."

"I don't always know what you like, Ravena." He fired the cheroot and the smoke was blue in the air, forming a question mark, a silent symbol of the question in her heart.

"Ravena –" He spoke her name and then glanced frowningly at the fountain. It was unlike him to be irresolute, and she felt more than ever certain that what he had to say involved their future together. Until now he had been relentless about everything. You will marry me, he had said. You will learn to live with this face of mine. . . .

Her eyes dwelt on his face, and it was strange how little his scars mattered. Because he never bowed his head and tried to hide them, they faded into insignificance and only his force, his pride, and his fine eyes mattered.

"What is it, Mark?" Her hands clenched together and she thought of her own words up in the mountains; her own declaration that they would never find real happiness with one another.

"I have to go away for about a week." The words sounded final and echoing in the *grotta*. "I am not going to tell you why, or where, but when I return there are things we must talk about – facts we must face."

She stared at him. "Can't we talk about them now?" She asked. "Do I have to wait another week –?"

"Yes." He rose to his feet and began to pace back and forth across the tiled floor. He drew hard on his cheroot and the smoke veiled his eyes. "I have asked a lot of you, Ravena, now I ask for your patience –"

"My patience, Mark? A week in which to wait and wonder, while you go off somewhere." Her green eyes blazed in her pale face like jewels. "Is this a business trip?"

He hesitated. "Not exactly."

Her heart beat rapidly. "Has it anything to do with that girl – the dark-haired girl who danced for you last night?"

"For me?" His dark eyes flashed to meet hers. "You think –"

"I know." Ravena felt cold, and forcibly composed as she looked at him. "I know you are involved with that girl, and that it's because of her you are going away. Mark, we don't have to wait a week to discuss our future – it can be discussed right now. If you go, then don't expect to find me here when you return."

"You will be here." His mouth was grim as he stepped towards her. "I insist on your promise that you will wait for me."

"Why insist on a promise?" She was trembling from the coldness inside her. "Donna Jocasta can always lock me in my room."

"Don't be childish!" His scars were etched lividly against his sun-dark skin. "All I ask of you is your trust for a single week – can't you give me that, at least?"

"At least?" she echoed. "I thought I had given you everything you asked of me – I am sorry it meant so little to you. It meant a great deal of pain to me, to be wrenched from my home and brought here to this – this house of shadows and memories. Do you think I ever called this place my home? Do you think I have spent one really happy day here? Do you think I care, Mark, whether you tell me now, or in a week's time, that the vendetta is played out?"

Now she was standing, and the green shadows of the *grotta* were in her eyes as she looked straight up at him, slim and uncaring of the strength in his lean, leashed body.

"Yes," he said, "the vendetta is played out. There are words left to say, but by the devil I won't say them now. I don't think I could."

He turned aside from her and his profile was etched against the green light ... cold, distant, proud. "I wish I could make you understand that this trip is both important, and curiously unimportant, but I must go because I have promised. Won't you promise me –"

"No," she said coldly. "No, Mark."

"*Che sarà sarà.*" He shrugged his wide shoulders and walked out of the *grotta* and Ravena gazed after him with his name frozen on her lips. *What will be, will be.*

The bandage about Ravena's ankle felt like a fetter that would not let her move from this spot beside the tinkling fountain. A fish darted, a petal fell, and the shadows crept nearer. *What will be, will be,* and she did nothing to alter the course of events. She stood chained there by pride, and let him go to that other girl.

La nonna must have suspected that a rift had opened between her grandson and his wife, but she made no mention of his abrupt departure from the house.

In the *salottino* that evening she talked of her days on the island, and of Mark's father, who had been a *maquis* leader during the war. "Understand a Sard and then you can call yourself a woman." She gazed keenly at Ravena, who felt cold and was sitting near the fire on the rug. "You sat like that the first evening you came here, child. I looked at the firelight on your hair and I thought to myself – ah, trouble! This one has red hair and green eyes and that means plenty of spirit."

"You wanted docility," Ravena said, and she watched the resin in the logs break into tiny spurts of flame.

"I wanted only happiness for Markos after so much grieving. I thought the grieving would kill him, or drive him mad ... tell me, Ravena, when will you tell him there is to be another child?"

Ravena looked up sharply. She wanted to deny what *la nonna* had guessed, but saw from the keen and jetty eyes that denial would be foolish. *La nonna* had seen too much of life, she realized what Mark had not dreamed of ... that Ravena might be carrying his son. The son to replace Dresti.

Sudden tears shone in Ravena's eyes. "What does it matter?" she said. "You were right from the very beginning, *la nonna*, you said that like should marry like. I am going away –"

"You cannot!" *La nonna* looked shocked. "There is to be a child – perhaps a son for Markos."

"And I don't count – as a person! I am here to provide Mark with what *he* wants, but my feelings are as nothing! It doesn't concern me that he has fallen in love with someone else!"

"What is that you say?" *La nonna* reached out and touched the tears on Ravena's cheek, as if to feel was to believe. "How can there be someone else? Markos married you –"

"And now he regrets it." Ravena gave a bitter little laugh. "*Nonna*, our marriage is over and I am going away."

"This is your home." The rings on the elderly hand bit into Ravena's fingers as she clutched the girl's hand. "All the di Curzio children are born in the house of the cypress, and this is where your child will be born."

"My child will be born at Ravenhall." Ravena rose to her feet and the folds of her dress fell gracefully about her figure that was still lissom and girlish. "Don't you know that tonight Mark is with another woman? She is of this island, as you all wanted. She is dark-haired, like Donata. Perhaps with her, Mark will find again what he has lost."

"My child, be reasonable."

"Reasonable?" Ravena closed her eyes and the whole sequence of her marriage flashed before her, scene after scene. Mark and herself at the altar – strangers. His hand pressing hers on the hilt of Guardy's sword as they cut the wedding cake. His face so dark in the hall at Ravenhall when she returned from her talk with Rhodri ... Mark carrying her up the stairs to the Knight's Tower ... kissing her in the tall grass yesterday and making her respond to a kiss that had been a deception.

Mark, telling her in the *grotta* that he was going away for a week, and admitting his involvement with the girl from the *trattoria*.

"I have been more reasonable than most would have been," she said quietly. "I can't be reasonable about this affair of Mark's –"

"There is no affair!" *La nonna* suddenly looked very old, and very tired. "Your husband, my child, has gone to find Marcu Cristi, and it means going into the hill country where the bandits hide out. He did not wish you to know. He swore me to secrecy. These men are lawless, but the girl begged him to find her young man, and he said it would please *you* if Virtuella's son could be persuaded to come home and lead a sensible life."

Slowly, one by one, the words penetrated Ravena's heart. "Oh, why didn't he tell me?" She thought of him in the *grotta*, looking so stony and proud as he left her. "Why make a secret of it?"

"Perhaps he thought you would worry – or perhaps he feared that you wouldn't." His grandmother looked sardonic, but her hand shook slightly as she gestured at the sideboard where the decanters stood. "Will you pour me a glass of wine, child? I feel a need of it, and from the look of your face you had better join me."

They drank their wine beside the fire, and the room was quiet except for the ticking of the clock and the purring of the logs. Darkness surrounded the house, with the cypress trees for its sentinels. Darkness lay over the hill and the wooded gorges, and Mark was out there somewhere and gone out of reach was the moment when she could have said: "I spoke in haste, Mark. There have been days, and nights, when I have felt with you a happiness to which I dare not give a name."

"Drink your wine," said his grandmother. "It will help you to sleep – tomorrow things will look better."

In the morning the sun was overclouded, but Ravena felt restless and she went walking in the lemon groves, and was half tempted to call on Virtuella. But no. It was better to wait and see what developed before building up hopes that might have no foundation, and Ravena returned to the Casa carrying a small bunch of the bright yellow flowers that grew – like hope – in the shade of the lemon trees.

A couple of days later the flowers had faded and were drooping in their vase, and Ravena was about to throw them away when there was a tap on her bedroom door. She opened the door and there was Renzio, holding out a letter which had just arrived for her. In the corner was a cluster of English stamps, and sprawled across the envelope the rather boyish handwriting of Rhodri Brenin.

"Would the *signora* like a cup of coffee?" Renzio was looking at her with a shade of anxiety.

"Yes, in the *grotta*, please. I'll read my letter there."

But she stood beside the fountain for a long moment just fingering the envelope, afraid to open it, afraid of what it might contain. She glanced about her, as if seeking a certain tall figure, and then with fingers that felt cold and clumsy she opened the letter.

Rhodri wrote to say that he was returning to Australia, and he had persuaded his father to go with him. The doctor was of the opinion that the sea voyage – they would go by ship – would be good for him, and now Ravena was married and living in Sardinia with her husband, there was no sound reason for keeping Ravenhall. The house was up for sale, and they expected to hear any time from their agent that it had been sold.

Ravena sat down slowly in a wicker chair, for her legs felt nerveless. Guardy was selling Ravenhall and going with Rhodri to New South Wales! So far away that it was out of her reach, out of her life, so that she felt abandoned by those who had been so close to her.

Her child, she had said only a few nights ago, would be born at Ravenhall, but even as she read Rhodri's letter the house in which she had spent her own childhood might be in the hands of a stranger.

She felt like weeping, for there seemed nothing left to cling to. No guardian, no home ... no one she felt sure of. Then she heard footsteps approaching and told herself a cup of coffee was better than nothing.

She glanced up to accept it, and there in the doorway stood a tall figure with tired, quizzical, searching eyes.

"Mark!"

"I thought you were going away," he half-smiled.

She flinched as if struck, for nothing in Rhodri's letter hurt as much as those few words from Mark. "*La nonna* told me why you had gone into the hills – among the bandits!"

"Don't tell me you were anxious?" He quirked an eyebrow and lounged in the doorway, dust on his knee-boots, a rent in his shirt, his hands in the pockets of his breeches.

"Did you find Virtuella's son?" she asked, and her fingers unaware were ripping Rhodri's letter into fragments. "Did you talk to him?"

"Yes. He needed someone to tell him that he was a young fool, that he had a mother and a girl waiting at home to give him their love ... something you can't beg, borrow or steal. I envy him."

Ravena glanced up from the torn pieces of Rhodri's letter. "Because the girl loves him?"

"Yes. Despite being hurt and disillusioned ... she loves him. Ravena, you are tearing that letter to shreds!"

She looked at the pieces in surprise. "It was from Rhodri."

"Rhodri?" Mark straightened to his full height and his eyes had a dangerous glint. "And you tore it up? Why?"

"I – I never noticed. He's going to Australia again, and Guardy is going with him. They're selling Raven-hall."

"So you will have nowhere to run home to?"

"Oh, Mark!" She put her face in her hands, for he was being so unfeeling and she had hoped – hoped for what? A tremor ran through her as in a stride he came to her and his hands touched her shoulders.

"Do you want to go to Australia?" he asked.

She felt him near to her and she realized exactly what she wanted, to be taken into his arms, to be held, and wanted by him.

"Ravena," his breath stirred her hair, "do you want to be free of me?"

She looked up at him and she knew she would never be free of him; that there was no running away from love because it was in your own heart. In that sense she could not choose to be free, but she could no longer stay with him – unloved.

"Will you let me go?" she asked.

"I won't make you stay – not if you don't want to. Not if my kisses and my scars are hateful to you." He drew away from her and for the first time he put up a hand and covered his ravaged cheek, and his eyes clouded with pain. "How could I ask you to love me – how dared I hope that you might learn to be tolerant? I had no rose garden to offer you, only a house of shadows and memories."

He was turning away when she came fully alive to what he had said. She jumped to her feet and cried his name. "Mark – darling!"

He stood very still, where a mass of purple clematis draped a trellis. His head was dark and proud against the flowers, and he wouldn't turn to look at her. She had to go and look straight up at him.

"Your kisses and your scars are not hateful to me," she said softly, and she reached up and drew his head down and her lips were soft in a kiss against his scarred cheek. "Love is more than skin deep, Mark."

"How long –?" He looked so unsure, and so endearing to her in that uncertainty.

"I don't know," she fingered the rent in his shirt. "Always – it feels as if I loved you always."

"You hated me!" He took hold of her and held her and she could feel his heart beating. "You married me so I wouldn't hurt your precious Rhodri. You went to him on our wedding day –"

"Guardy had been ill. I was afraid of what it would do to him if Rhodri told him about – about the car crash. Rhodri wanted to tell him – it took me hours to talk him out of it."

"It would have freed you from any obligation to me," Mark said, and even as he spoke he drew her even closer to him. "Do you suppose you didn't wish to be free?"

She put her arms about his neck, she looked into his eyes, and then in shyness she pressed her face against him, and the fountain made silvery music beside them. "I didn't really know what I wanted then, but I know what I want now. I want to try and make you happy, Mark. Even happier than Donata made you –"

His hands bit into her waist, forcing a gasp from her lips. "I married Donata to please my family," he said. "I married you to please myself. I would have let nothing and nobody stand in my way. I thought I had a right to you, because of the way I lost Dresti. I can hardly believe that now I have your love."

"You have more, my dear." She stood on tiptoe and whispered a certain secret in his ear, and after that it was a long time before either of them spoke.

Soon the shadows would lift from the house of the cypress, and the laughter of a child would be heard there again. Ravena would watch lovingly as her husband lifted the boy on to his shoulder and looked at her with brilliant loving eyes.

Che sarà sarà.

🌹 Mills & Boon
Best Seller Romances

The very best of Mills & Boon Romances, brought back for those of you who missed reading them when they were first published.

Each month we bring back four great romantic titles. Look out for the latest issues.

Best Seller romances are also available from the Mills & Boon Reader Service. You can have all four delivered to your home each month, post and packing free.

For full details write to:

Best Seller Romances, Mills & Boon Reader Service, P.O. Box 236, Croydon, Surrey CR9 3RU.

The 🌹 Mills & Boon rose is the rose of romance.